things are good now

things are good now

stories

DJAMILA IBRAHIM

Published in Canada in 2018 by House of Anansi Press Inc.
www.houseofanansi.com

House of Anansi Press is committed to protecting our natural environment. As part of our efforts, the interior of this book is printed on paper that contains 100% post-consumer recycled fibres, is acid-free, and is processed chlorine-free.

22 21 20 19 18   1 2 3 4 5

Library and Archives Canada Cataloguing in Publication

Ibrahim, Djamila, 1975–
[Short stories. Selections]
Things are good now / Djamila Ibrahim.

Issued in print and electronic formats.
ISBN 978-1-4870-0188-9 (softcover).—ISBN 978-1-4870-0190-2
(EPUB).—ISBN 978-1-4870-0191-9 (Kindle)

I. Title.

PS8617.B73A6 2018   C813'.6   C2017-901299-1
                  C2017-901300-9

Book design: Alysia Shewchuk

We acknowledge for their financial support of our publishing program the Canada Council for the Arts, the Ontario Arts Council, and the Government of Canada through the Canada Book Fund.

Printed and bound in Canada

For my parents

contents

little copper bullets

THE DAY THE FIGHTER JETS CAME, AISHA WAS sitting on the floor between her mother's legs. The backs of her own folded knees itched from the sweat built up in the creases. Her mother dug into her scalp with an afro comb to draw straight lines. Then, with assured quick movements, she grabbed strands of Aisha's hair with her calloused hands and plaited it into tight braids. "Stay still," she ordered now and then. "You're not a child anymore. You are a young woman." Her voice softened to a whisper although they were alone in the small, one-room hut they shared with Aisha's father and her three siblings. Aisha hated being reminded she'd become a young woman, especially since her betrothal: the new responsibilities and restrictive rules, her fiancé's large family watching her every move, their apprehensive whispers and furtive, appraising looks. It all made her feel like she'd turned into a time bomb overnight.

That's when they heard the deafening noise and, almost instantaneously, felt the ground trembling beneath them as if the might and weight of the heavens had fallen right outside their door. Aisha saw only a moment's confusion in her mother's kohled eyes before her mother dragged her under the only bed in the room. They lay there for a long time, Aisha's cheek against the ground, the taste of dust from the dirt floor in her mouth. Her mother's body half on top of hers made it hard for her to breathe. They prayed. Aisha recited a succession of Quranic verses she'd memorized from her father's lips, jumping from *surah* to *surah*, the continuous flow of mysterious, holy words forming a glue that prevented her heart from shattering in her chest.

That day, the village buried forty people in a mass grave. Aisha's father, who had been herding his few goats toward their clan's grazing land when the Soviet-made, Ethiopian MiGs bombed the village, was one of them. The next night, Aisha and four of her friends, all around thirteen or fourteen years old, left the village to join the Eritrean freedom fighters in the mountains. They travelled on foot, crossing for the first time the lowlands of their birth by the Red Sea all the way into the Sahel highlands of Eritrea. Seventeen years later, in 1994, Aisha took another journey, this time to a new life in Canada.

"HELLO, AISHA," Jamil, the convenience store owner says, extending a fat hand from behind the counter to shake hers. "How are you?"

"Hi, Jamil. I'm good. Du Maurier Light, please."

"Hey, Aisha," says Michael, his shiny bald head sticking out between two revolving stands of greeting cards and newspapers.

"Oh, hi, Michael. I didn't see you there, hiding behind your newspaper."

"I should make him pay for the free knowledge he's getting, but my heart is too big," Jamil says with a thick South Asian accent. He picks up a plastic stool from a corner and brings it closer to the counter. The seat disappears under his wide body.

"You know I can find these at the public library a few blocks away, right?" Michael says, with a hint of a Jamaican accent. He folds the newspaper, puts it back on the shelf, and comes around to the front of the store.

"I don't think so. Probably old ones from last year," Jamil says, flicking his hand in dismissal.

"This shows you have never set foot in a library, old man," Michael says.

"I went to library all the time back home," Jamil says. "I ask you, do you even have libraries in Jamaica?"

He slides the back of one hand against the palm of the other to show the emptiness of Michael's argument. "And who you calling old anyway? Have you seen your bald head?" Jamil adds, running his fingers through his thick grey hair. He winks at Aisha with a proud grin on his face.

Aisha doesn't mind the old man's shameless flirtations. She sometimes even feeds them, holding her own against the men's squabbles and teasings. But not today. She leans against the glass counter under which colourful instant lottery tickets are displayed and listens with a quiet smile as the men argue and laugh. The rhythm and depth of their friendship is delicious to her ear. It reminds her of her early childhood, her large family, their gossip and banter, the idyllic, lively scenes forged in a time of peace.

She spent twelve years in the Eritrean resistance army where, in makeshift classrooms, moving from base to base, against a backdrop of gunfire, she learned to read and write. She learned about her country's history, the roles old empires and powerful modern nations played in shaping her life. She learned to believe in and fight for an ideal bigger than herself. On a vast flat land of golden earth and blue mirage, and on the blisteringly cold mountaintops, she learned to use weapons. In the folds of damp caves, she practised facing fear, pain, and death; she prepared herself for capture, torture, and rape. And for the faltering of will.

That's where she'd first met Yosef, amid the bombardments of their base in Af'abet. With the passion and decisiveness of wartime hearts, she and Yosef fell in love and married within a couple of months—he, a city bourgeois educated in the USSR; she, a girl from a small tribe of semi-nomads in the Semhar lowlands. But it was wartime, and the rebels observed the tenets of socialist equality full-heartedly. He was the patient comrade who'd opened her mind and eyes to the world beyond the narrow boundaries of her upbringing. The man from whose husky voice she had savoured flows of ideas ancient and new; the man with whom she dreamed a nation into being. In the secrecy of her mind, Aisha had felt grateful to the invisible hand of history, and even to war, for having brought them together.

After the liberation, she and Yosef settled down in Asmara. As a reward for his service in the armed struggle, he was granted a job in government. She was not so lucky. She was one of the tens of thousands of demobilized female fighters left out of the redistributions of national resources and government jobs granted to the male rebels. But to complain or show dejection was considered unpatriotic, a testament to one's reluctance to step up to the difficult work of building a country. Worse, to Aisha, it was akin to insulting the memory of the hundreds of thousands of men and women who'd lost their lives in the conflict, some of whom had been like family to her. So she settled for a volunteer position teaching illiterate women to write and read while she studied English in the evenings in the hope that a diploma would eventually get her a paying job.

Then one day she heard Yosef's mother plead with her son: "That was wartime, my son. You don't need a drunk for a wife. She doesn't even try to be discreet about it. She drinks in plain sight, like a man. Please, put an end to this." Aisha stood outside the small house, her hand on the doorknob for a moment, before retracing her steps out of the compound and into the neighbourhood bar she and Yosef frequented. She'd seen it happen too many times. Female fighters deemed valuable and admirable in the field were seen, in times of peace, as too hard-headed and independent to make good wives and mothers. Her own family had threatened to disown her for marrying outside of her tribe and faith, too, but she could handle them. Yosef, though, she couldn't be sure. She didn't wait to see him succumb to the pressures of family and tradition. She left him before he could leave her.

"Anyway, forget about this old man," Michael says and turns to Aisha. "So, Adam said you're going back to your country."

Michael's inquisitive eyes startle Aisha out of her memories. She nods and smiles, a slow stretch of her closed mouth. At times it was still hard, even for her, to believe she was going to leave the safety and peace Canada had afforded her in the last four years to go back and enlist in the Eritrean army. And as she'd expected, her boyfriend, Adam, had reacted badly to the news that she would be defending her country against Ethiopia's second invasion.

Since they'd met last year at Habesha Restaurant on Rideau Street, Adam had been adamant that they could be together.

"So what if you're Eritrean and I'm Ethiopian? We're not the first couple in history to deal with a divided allegiance," he'd said when she first told him why she couldn't date him. She didn't want to explain herself any further — there were no words to convey what wars do to people's hearts, what a life sheathed in death does to the mind. Besides, she loathed civilians' curiosity. How could they expect her to explain what it was like to pick up pieces of your friends, to try to remember the sound of their laughter or the shape of their eyes and instead only recall a mangled neck or guts spilling out? These things couldn't be shared with anyone, not even your comrades. There was always a disconnect, even within the Eritrean community, between her experiences and people's assumptions of war, what they expect an ex-fighter to be like and who she was.

Adam wanted to know about her time in the field, too; she could see it in his eyes. But he had a strong sense of propriety that put her at ease. He gave her room to be her own woman, not a heroine or a spitfire. Later, as she let herself go into his embrace, as she let the smell and sound of him permeate her pores, she was aware of a wall between them, an ever-caving and brittle one, but a wall nonetheless. With time, he became the lover she desired, the companion she trusted, and the raft she hung onto when she felt as if she were drowning. But some things are hard to share and some walls are hard to overcome. So when she heard about the new war, her thoughts rushed to him. She saw the wall reinforce itself between them. The realization of imminent loss was immediate, almost instinctive. Pain paralyzed her mind and body for days. Before she told him of her decision, she mourned the end of something that was never fully theirs.

"Yes, I am going back. And I heard what you told Adam," Aisha says to Michael.

Adam had relayed their conversation to her. "Forget Aisha, it's her loss. Go out and meet new people, son. You might stumble on The One sooner than you think," Michael had advised Adam. Michael has been married to a Jamaican woman for twenty years. He hardly ever says anything good about his wife but he always calls her The One. "You see, I can't stand that woman, but I can't be with another. I think she has some Haitian voodoo shit on me, man," he had explained once.

"Poor Adam," Jamil says, shaking his head with exaggeration.

"You told him to find himself a white lady, didn't you?" Aisha asks, searching Jamil's face for a sign of surprise.

"No, no, I didn't say that..."

When Adam had first introduced her to Jamil, he'd said, "Jamil has spent so much time imagining how things would have been different if he'd immigrated to Canada without a wife and children that he has come to believe in the possibility of a Don Juan version of himself. That dream now lives among his most cherished possessions and accomplishments."

Michael laughs, his strong, fat-covered body shaking. "No way. White women are trouble. When they leave you, they take everything—your children, your money, everything. I told Adam to find a woman from his own country. And that's only if he can't convince you to stay," he says to Aisha's inquiring eyes. "Why do you want to go back anyway?"

Adam had neglected to tell her this part of the story. Why? Did Michael's suggestion appeal to him? What if it confirmed Adam's pre-existing plans? She feels her blood boil, her stomach sour. After all that talk about building a life together. After all those nights they spent at Habesha Restaurant: she, teaching him to synchronize his steps to the beats of Tigrigna songs and he, showing her how to shake her shoulders to the rhythm of Amharic music. Did he wish she were Ethiopian, then, that he didn't have to teach her these things?

"It's my home," she says. "That's why. Anyway, yes. I came to say goodbye." She extends a stiff hand across the counter and suddenly feels claustrophobic in the dim convenience store.

Michael has put into words what she had always feared, and this provokes an irrational hatred toward him. That she was the one who'd decided to leave Adam did not ease her jealousy; it just made her anger unfocused, more volatile.

"I was just joking, Aisha. You know that, right?" Jamil says, both of his hands covering hers.

"Be good now," Michael says, pointing at her. He steps closer, past her extended hand, and wraps her body with his. She stays stiff for a moment before giving in.

"Have a nice trip, Aisha. And good luck," Jamil says, craning his head toward the door as she leaves the store.

AISHA STOPS AT a red light across from her nineteen-storey building. She looks up at the lifeless grey assemblage of shabby concrete and metal.

"This building would be a great setting for a remake of George Orwell's 1984," Adam had told her once, a couple of months after they started dating.

She'd looked at him with questioning eyes. Adam has always tried to kindle a passion for art and literature in her. She loves the way his eyes light up when he talks about these things, the way he meshes worlds and ideas together and transforms them into fantastic or touching stories, but she prefers tangible, real-life events to fiction. She once told him she admired Margaret Thatcher. The next day, he bought her *The Collected Speeches of Margaret Thatcher.* She looked at the picture on the cover for a moment: the Iron Lady's chin between her motherly fingers, her mouth slightly open as if, after much deliberation, she were about to utter a condemning sentence. When she first learned about Thatcher, Aisha was in the field and had believed she too could pursue a career in government after the war—Aisha was often praised for her leadership skills on the battleground. But she'd quickly found out after independence that political clout, and marriage and family were two almost contradictory aspirations for an Eritrean woman to entertain. When Aisha looked up from the book to thank Adam, she found in his eager smile the look that her ex-husband wore when he was excited about something. Her past had superimposed itself on the man standing before her. Although Adam and Yosef looked nothing alike, the vision bothered her for days, made her wonder if people changed at all or if they always fell for the same person over and over again.

ADAM SWIVELS HIS chair around to face the glass wall of his sixteenth-floor cubicle. He stretches his long legs on the moss-green industrial carpet and rests his clasped hands on his stomach. It's 4:30 p.m. on a Friday and he has not met his weekly quota of processed passport applications. This would have bothered him a year ago. These days, it only aggravates his overall weariness. His thoughts dissolve into the piece of grey sky trapped between some of Ottawa's tallest buildings. He wonders if he could still dissuade Aisha from leaving or if he's crazy for thinking of it.

He has tried many times to imagine Aisha in the field, her life as a freedom fighter. He has tried to picture a younger version of the Aisha he knows climbing semi-arid mountains, an AK-47 slung on her shoulder, ammunition dangling around her waist and across her chest, or squatting for days in camouflaged trenches, hiding from fighter jets as they hunted for targets like hooded vultures above a rocky terrain. He'd composed this collage of images from documentaries he'd watched and an old black-and-white picture of her she'd shown him once of a dark-skinned young woman in khaki fatigues under a frankincense tree, rifle by her side, offering the photographer a wide smile of slightly protruding teeth and squinting eyes framed by a wild afro. But he can't extrapolate. Especially when he thinks of the hundreds of thousands of Ethiopian soldiers who died in that thirty-year-long war. Sometimes an irrational fear consumes him. What if he finds out someone he grew up with had died from her bullets? Maybe Girma, his neighbour, or Abye, his cousin. What if she'd been an interrogator? All kinds of war crimes are exposed on the news all the time. These thoughts cause sweat to build up in his armpits and on his palms, and wipe his mind blank. He always veers back to reason though. *Our countries were at war*, he tells himself. *She did what she had to do.*

Last week, when Aisha told him of her decision to return to Eritrea, he thought it would pass. After all, Aisha was always on the brink of going back. Every time things got tough, she'd argue she preferred the hardship of her homeland to the daily little humiliations she suffered in Canada.

"Four years in this country, Adam. Four years, I've been trying," she'd say, four fingers unfolding from under dry knuckles for emphasis. "I've cleaned bloody filth off hospital sheets, washed floors, windows," she'd list. "Taken orders from racist fools. And nothing in my hands. Nothing."

Adam would try to appease her with the tale of his own difficult debut as a new immigrant from Ethiopia eighteen years ago, but she'd dismiss him with a groan.

This time, she had a different reason.

"Ethiopia has invaded Eritrea again," she said without looking at him, her voice cold and taut, as though she'd always known this turn of events was inevitable.

"Well, that's a matter of perspective," he wanted to say, but he knew this would have led to the same ardent and usually fruitless arguments border disputes elicit the world over.

When he was a kid, he used to think there was a secret meaning to the fact that the old Ethiopian map resembled Africa's map but upside down. A secret he hoped to one day elucidate. And even now, whenever he looks at Ethiopia's new map, drawn after Eritrea's separation, it always jars him a little that he doesn't instantly recognize it, that it no longer reflects his childhood's fantasy.

His eyes followed Aisha as her hips, shaped like elongated parentheses, strode past him from her small kitchen to her equally small living room. Like all the times he'd gone without smoking for days only to be lulled back into the habit by the slightest whiff of cigarette smoke in the air, the waft of her perfume, a mysterious blend of sandalwood and citrus, invaded his mind with desire. He wished he could erase both their histories.

She placed bowls of the *sega wet* he'd brought and the lentil sauce she'd made beside the tray of *injera* on the coffee table and sat across from him, a bottle of Heineken in her hands, her face in the shadow of a big lush tropical plant she'd found limp and dry in her building's garbage collection room.

"I'm going back," she said.

"What? Why?"

"I'm going to fight, what else?" she said, her voice ringing with the clarity of a revolutionary mind, her plum-coloured thick lips quivering a little.

He held her stare for a moment. Aisha's short afro looked thinner and tamer than in her picture from the field. A few greys coiled around her ears.

Usually, on Saturday nights, they'd meet up for dinner and drinks at Habesha Restaurant which, on weekends after 11 p.m., turned into a nightclub of sorts. The owner would dim the lights and remove some of the tables in the centre of the room to make space for a dance floor. Aisha and Adam would sometimes catch some of the Eritrean patrons staring at them as they danced or hear them make sideways remarks in Tigrigna that Aisha would translate for him.

Some days, if Aisha had had a few drinks, she'd lash out: "You were sitting on your asses fattening your guts and wallets here while I was on the field fighting for your rights. How dare you judge me?"

Adam's conservative upper-middle-class upbringing didn't prepare him for vociferous public altercations. His was a childhood steeped in intellectual pursuit, and the vague concepts of honour and manhood he'd been taught always gave precedence to reason. But in those instances where alcohol got the best of him, these teachings would quickly make room for something else. When Aisha started fights, he'd feel invigorated, given a chance to prove his valour as a man. He would stand a little to the side, or stay still in his chair without looking directly at anybody, but displaying just enough physical presence to show his readiness to defend her if needed.

"Aye, yene jegna," he'd say to her later as they stumbled their way home, touched by the ardour of her feelings for him and proud to be in a relationship with such a bold, unflinching woman. Even though he'd never admit it to anybody, Aisha's indomitable spirit excited him. It aroused in him a desire to make her fierceness his. Sometimes, he even envied her history.

Adam wondered whether Aisha's decision to go back and fight stemmed from an unarticulated wish to reunite with her ex-husband, and to reignite what they'd had in the field.

"Don't you think you're a little too old to be toting machine guns and living in caves and trenches again?" he said. The bluntness of his words surprised him, but he hated the thought that Aisha and Yosef fitted into each other's lives in a way she and he never could.

"I can still help my country. Here, I'm nothing," Aisha said. A hint of sorrow seeped through her voice.

"That's not true. Here you don't risk your life. You have people who care about you..." Elbows on his knees, his lanky body bent forward, he scratched the label off the Heineken bottle, hoping to find a revelation beneath it. He was never one to express his feelings or speak his mind freely. This frustrated him. "You already gave twelve years of your life to your country. What did it give you in exchange, huh?" he continued. He washed down the nebulous mix of anger and despair with beer.

When he looked across the coffee table again, Aisha's hazel eyes burnt a hole in the space where his anger was. This always caught him by surprise, the way her eyes could turn into little copper bullets without a moment's notice.

"I'm sorry, Aisha, I didn't mean to say . . . It's just that . . ." He gulped down his drink.

They talked about African politics, of course: a coup here, a tribal war there, the questionable involvement of this or that Western government, the kinship of a bloody history and an antidote to the austere alienness of the world outside their doorsteps. But they made sure to stay clear of the politics involving their two countries. Whenever something happened in one or the other nation, they would support each other's frustration with, "Well, that's Africa for you." And if it was good news, they'd say, "Let's wait and see. I'm sure someone will manage to fuck that up." But the new reality couldn't be brushed off as easily. Adam realized then how much simpler it had been to deal with the idea of their countries' war in past tense. "The past is the past," he'd imagined himself saying to her as soon as he'd mustered the courage to ask her to move in with him. Now, even if she wasn't going back . . . He felt as if he were standing in the middle of a rickety wooden bridge, watching the ropes unravel from both sides.

"I'm tired of cleaning washrooms all day long. Eating, sleeping, a never-ending succession of empty days," she said.

He looked at her in silence.

"I'm a fighter, a soldier, Adam. War, privation, that was hard, but if I stay here I'll go crazy," she said and sighed.

He knew her last words held some truth he'd avoided. He had seen the anger she hid behind a veil of cigarette smoke, the rootlessness in her eyes masked by a frozen stare, the ugly head of depression quickly drowned in hard liquor and petty fights. Having spent most of her life fighting a blood-and-flesh enemy, Aisha was at a loss when confronted with the daily wars of a mundane life.

"There is so much you can do for your people right here, Aisha. Here is an idea: If real engagement is what you're seeking, why don't you volunteer at the Catholic Immigration Centre?" he said, holding her gaze. "The government provides refugees with financial and logistical assistance, but the psychological impact of violence these people bring with them — who is better placed to provide that kind of support than you?"

She looked at him blankly, as though she had already gone.

HE WALKS TO the glass wall across from his cubicle and stretches his arms, bending his body sideways to free the knots of sedentary life stuck in his lower back. With his hands in his pockets, he watches rush hour traffic below. People in dark suits scurry in and out of the slice of Bank Street visible from his vantage point. He remembers how excited he was when he first got hired at the passport office. After five years working as a janitor cleaning movie theatres and community centres, and five more as a parking lot attendant, he'd finally graduated from university and secured his first permanent job. "A federal government position. You are moving up in the world, my friend," people had said, patting his shoulder. Sure, running around the office locating misplaced files and archiving others was not what his English literature degree had promised, but everybody seemed to agree it was just a matter of time before he'd climb up the ladder.

"You are set for life, brother," his old cleaning buddies had said. "Job security, pension, paid vacations..." They counted until they ran out of fingers, pride on their breaths, envy in their eyes.

Now, eight years and three promotions later, he spends his days stooped over a never-ending pile of army-green files, processing passport application forms: examining birth certificates, matching photos to IDs, evaluating eligibility, carrying out reference checks, and answering queries from applicants.

"Veal-fattening pen," he mumbles to his reflection, repeating Douglas Coupland's words. "Mine comes with a view. I must be moving up in life indeed."

He watches his body suspended mid-air in the glass wall, melting in the reflection of office furniture and the world outside. He enjoys this fragmented, washed-out image of himself. It gives him access to another plane of existence, an alternate reality where he can draw his life's path with intention and structure — something he finds impossible to fathom in front of a mirror's glaring constraints. He imagines himself convincing Aisha to stay or at least to postpone her trip. The UN has started mediations already; maybe this new war will end quickly. He has enough for a down payment on a house. They could start a family.

"Head in the clouds again, eh?" Mark says, peeking over the light green cubicle divider between his and Adam's workstations. His pink button-down shirt accentuates his face's usual ruddiness, turning his chubby, smooth cheeks a grapefruit red.

"Um. Just rearranging the furniture in my imaginary palace. Did you say something?" Adam says, returning to his desk.

"Pat and I are going for drinks. Do you wanna come?"

Pat waves from two rows away. His thick, slick brown hair glistens under the light above his head, and taut muscles protrude from under his short-sleeved white dress shirt.

"Everything about Pat says boisterous and vain," Adam had said to Mark the first and only time Adam agreed to go to a nightclub with these two co-workers. Pat had volunteered to teach the two men how to pick up women. In the end, Adam and Mark had spent the night with their backs against the bar's sticky counter, guzzling down one beer after another, the contrast between their physiques accentuating the banality of their looks while Pat prowled around the crowded room making out with one woman here, dancing to deafening beats with another there. "A cock in a hen pen," Mark had said, his face red from alcohol and jealousy.

Adam turns to examine the papers scattered on his desk and the stack of passport application files for a second.

"No. Not tonight, guys. I have things to do," he says and picks up his book and lunch box with quick, decisive gestures.

"Let me guess. Aisha again, right?" Pat says. "You're so whipped, man," he adds, his lips stretching over perfectly aligned, white teeth.

"Whatever you say, big guy. Anyway, have fun and don't do anything I wouldn't," Adam says as he heads toward the exit.

Before he met Aisha, he rarely turned down Friday nights at the pub. After work, he and a few of his co-workers would head to the Royal Oak or D'Arcy McGee's for a chance to blow off some steam, huddled around burgers, fries, and a continuous flow of beer. For a chance to meet women too. Some days, the memory of the fetid concoction of cigarette butts, fried foods, and stale beer would even trigger a subtle urge in him, something resembling hope and the fulfillment of desires, as though a cure to his most unspoken ache would finally materialize from one of these pubs' dark crevices. But these nights—he always realized this the next day—all ended the same way. He'd spend more money than he should, stagger home, wake up with a bad headache and foul breath, and, more often than not, alone.

A cool early-fall breeze greets him as he steps out the office building's revolving glass door. He wraps his black-and-grey-checkered wool scarf around his neck and walks toward the outdoor parking lot on Gilmour Street to his car. The business district has mostly emptied itself of the thousands of civil servants who roam the concrete, glass, and chrome landscape by day. Here and there, some tourists search for signs of open restaurants or hurry up and down Sparks Street in their thin jackets for a last-minute purchase of Canadian souvenirs. Adam loves fall: the sunburnt leaves reflecting the afternoon light, infusing the city with a tender shade of gold or flying about like confetti, defying life's precariousness. But today it's the naked trees that attract his attention, their branches like old arthritic fingers sprouting from calloused palms, prayerful. They echo his own desperate desire to delay the inevitable.

When he first came to Canada, he had felt as if everyone was looking at him. Back then, he used to walk with a heightened sense of having taken up space that was not his to take. He was apologetic and eager, too eager, to please. Then, when he realized he could never hide the sin of intrusion his blackness betrayed, he decided to find other ways to blend in. He sat at bus stops every day after work or in parks and coffee shops and observed white people's behaviour, taking notes of their mannerisms and imitating them in front of his washroom mirror at night. After a couple of years of struggling to conquer the English language, and because he'd always loved to read, he enrolled at Carleton University to study English literature. *Two birds with one stone*, he'd told himself, quoting from a thin book he found in a second-hand bookstore titled *1000 English Animal Idioms and Their Meanings*. He would try to figure out the logic behind expressions like "drunk as a skunk" and "busy as a beaver," then consult encyclopedias at the public library to find pictures of these strange animals. Almost two decades later, the language of his adopted country still sometimes feels like a rough, alien skin trapping his essence. But what scares him most is that the more he feels he's conquered the English language and the more he fits the mould of the successful, well-integrated immigrant, the more removed he becomes from the tangible experiences of his past, his memories unable to coexist with his present. With each step he took toward assimilation, with each hurdle he overcame to be just like everyone else, he'd slowly shed layers of himself, losing ground on something he can't put a finger on, becoming invisible to himself.

The smell of fried food from a nearby restaurant makes his stomach growl. He dreads seeing Aisha tonight. As her departure date approaches, his excitement about spending time with her has been riddled with intensifying anxiety. He almost wishes her gone so he could be relieved of the stress. He thinks of going to Habesha Restaurant for some *kitfo* or *tibs* instead, then quickly changes his mind. He shudders at the idea of spending his evening with lonely Ethiopian men who only come to life in dreams of long-dead revolutions, their language calcified in violence and sorrow. Besides, going there will make him miss Aisha. Her loud laughter, the way she dances with her eyes closed, the way she loves and hates with passion.

He has been having the same nightmare every night for the last two weeks. He is at the Meskel Square in Addis Ababa. At the centre of the square, Colonel Mengistu Haile Mariam stands onstage behind a cluster of microphones in front of a crowd of young people, cheering and clapping. The old Ethiopian dictator picks up a bottle full of a red substance — Adam knows it's blood — from a nearby table, holds it above his head for the citizens to see, then bends down and smashes it against the stage. He does this again and again, an invisible hand providing him with new bottles. The entranced spectators cheer him on, getting louder with each broken bottle. Feeding on the public's frenzy, the blood swells before it crashes on the enchanted congregation, drowning them. Adam sees his old girl-friend, Mebrat, floating in a bubble of clear water by his feet, untainted by the pool of blood around them. He veers to the side to avoid stepping on her corpse, struggling to keep his balance. Sensing his panic, Mebrat opens her dead eyes. Adam wakes up gasping for air and drenched in sweat, then spends hours trying to clear his mind of the painful images of Mengistu's seventeen-year-long campaign of terror that took the life of his old girlfriend and so many of his childhood friends.

Last night, an idea struck him. He felt a semblance of understanding of what the dream might mean. An odd, jumbled-up sensation of déjà vu overtook him. He gave up on trying to go back to sleep and instead reached for the small tin he'd kept on the topmost shelf of his closet for years. As he went through pictures of his family, his childhood friends, and of Mebrat and him, he unearthed an old guilt. Mebrat became involved in the underground resistance against Mengistu's govern-ment to be closer to him, to impress him — she was only seventeen. Six months later, he had left her to her own devices when she refused to leave the organiza-tion and the country with him. He'd given up on her too easily. And now he might be giving up on Aisha the same way. But this new realization didn't help him find a way to keep Aisha from leaving. It just made the pain of losing her stronger and any hope of winning her over evaporate.

He unlocks his car door and drops his lunch box and book on the passenger seat. He stretches his arms behind his back and yawns before he puts his key into the ignition. He's tired of trying to convince Aisha to stay, but the alternative is a dark, empty space he can't allow himself to imagine yet. As he joins the traffic on Slater Street heading toward Aisha's apartment, he knows he will try again and again until she leaves.

AISHA CURVES HER body around the door and leans into the apartment for a last glance at what has been her home for three years. She can sense Adam watching her, his back against the hallway wall.

"Alright, I'm ready to go," she says, locking the door. She adjusts her overstuffed purse on her shoulder and, with long, determined steps, heads toward the visitor parking lot where Adam has parked his Honda Accord. Adam has already stored her two suitcases in the car.

"Let's have one last smoke before we head to the airport," he says as they step out of the apartment building. "It'll give you time to say goodbye to the neighbourhood."

Aisha turns her head toward him and quickly takes in his slim frame. Their eyes meet but there is nothing to say.

It is a little past six in the evening. The sky is a soothing blue except for the splash of turmeric across the sun. The aroma of charred meat from a nearby barbecue

competes with the acrid smell of their burning cigarettes. They lean against the back of Adam's car and
watch the eastern white pines at the end of the parking
lot wave their branches left and right to the rhythm of
the wind, like lovers swaying to an old, slow tune.

"Here, before I forget," Aisha says and hands him
her apartment keys to deliver to the rental office on
Monday.

"When it's nice out like this, it's easy to forget how
cold it gets in the winter," Adam says.

They hear the intermittent dribbling of a basketball
from the court on the west side of the building.

"You know what? I'll miss watching the snowfall
from my window," Aisha says, remembering the times
she sat watching the white flakes drift down in a constant and tender flow, smoothing out the knots of
anxiety in her chest. "Like thick balls of gutted pillow
silently blurring the boundary between earth and sky,"
Adam had said once.

"Sure, it's easier to miss snow when you know you
won't have to deal with the bitter cold anymore," Adam
says, smiling.

"Yes. That's how I want to remember it. I'll think of
black ice and frostbite when thirst and sunburn blister
my mind with pain. That and when I realize I can't run
the way I used to."

"Not with all the smoking you've been doing," Adam
teases again, nudging her elbow with his.

She looks into his eyes for a moment, as if he'd revealed a secret she didn't know he knew, then looks away.

"Did I ever tell you about my first snow experience?" she says, turning her whole body to face him again. "As you know, it was within days of moving to Ottawa that I landed my first cleaning job in that government building on Laurier Street." She points north. "The first day, I mopped vinyl floors and vacuumed carpets in the windowless basement. When I left the building, at the end of my shift at eight, the whole city was covered in white." The cigarette tucked between her fingers draws waves in the air. "It wasn't snowing anymore, so it was impossible to tell whether the white powder covering the ground, cars, and trees had descended from the sky or exploded out of the earth's entrails. All the landmarks I had painstakingly memorized to get home were erased. Only a white world under a black silent sky." She stops for a moment. "The terror I felt that night will stay with me forever," she says, chuckling. Grey puffs of smoke escape her lips.

"Are you going to stay in Asmara for long?" Adam asks.

She knows Adam wants to know about her ex-husband but won't ask.

"I don't know," she says. "I will report to the Ministry of Defence as soon as I can. Hopefully, I won't have to spend too much time in the city." She shudders at the thought of running into Yosef, of maybe finding out he has remarried and had children. But a part of her wants these things to be true so that she can keep Yosef in her past. She doesn't want to betray Adam. She worries about her brothers' reaction to her unannounced return. (Her mother had passed away while she was in the field.) Aisha didn't tell her siblings she was going back for fear they might try to dissuade her. They had grown too dependent on her financial assistance to understand what it took to earn the money she sent them every month. Now she wonders if she's made a mistake.

"What will you miss about Ottawa?"

She thinks for a moment.

"The radio program," she says. "I'll miss the radio station. I feel bad for having left Daniel stranded without a replacement."

"I'm sure he'll find someone else."

Daniel had said her voice was made for radio. "It's not a paid position, of course. It's only a one-hour slot on a multicultural program funded by the university, but your contribution would be very important to the community and to the Eritrean youth growing up here." His eyes were fixed on her like a puppy's. "Children born or raised in Canada don't have a clue about the Struggle, about the sacrifices people like yourself have made to free our country, so in a way you'd be our resident historian," he'd said. Aisha wondered what kind of a woman she would have been if she'd grown up in Canada. Would she have cared about what happened in Eritrea?

She thought about the East African youth who came to party at Habesha Restaurant after the other clubs closed, moving seamlessly between the larger Canadian world and the restaurant's more traditional setting and interacting with each other free of the politics of older *Habesha* patrons. They did these things as if exercising their birthright, casually, the way people who'd never had to ponder the meaning or price of rights would. "These kids just don't know how good they have it," Adam would say. "If I was a teenager growing up in Canada," she'd reply, laughing, "I'd probably break all the laws and rack up speeding tickets just for the thrill of it." Outside the glass walls of the DJ booth, students rushed from one building to another, along cement pathways criss-crossing the immaculate green lawns. Two young women were reading under a willow tree, thin leaves raining down on their shiny long hair and their books. Aisha loved the scenery. It made her feel cheerful. She thought of how energizing it would be to spend a couple of hours a week around so many learned people. *Maybe it's not too late. Maybe this is my chance to do something different. I could go back to school, get a better job*, she'd reasoned before she accepted the offer to host the program.

"May 24, 1991: the day our valiant men and women marched into Asmara — what had been the last bastion of the Ethiopian invaders," she'd announced the first day, trying to keep from accidentally pushing the buttons on the broadcasting console in front of her. "It was the best day of my life. Days-old sweat stains on my clothes, my face caked with dust and dirt that made it feel rough like bread crust, but none of that mattered. Nothing else in the world mattered. I was among thousands of my comrades. We entered Asmara in broad daylight, triumphant and proud. No more clandestine missions or furtive glances in the dark to avoid running into Ethiopian soldiers. All around us on Liberation Avenue, an ecstatic and incredulous population gathered to greet us with songs, ululation, and dancing. Old women waved palm leaves, little kids ran alongside our trucks, Jeeps, and tanks. Even the dust seemed to join in on the celebration. That's when it really hit me that the dream had materialized. We had become a free nation." Her voice was energized by the recollection of that day's events.

The callers were supportive at first. Then one day, a young woman called in. "Instead of bending our ears with glossy dreams, why are you not talking about the people rotting in prisons across Eritrea right now?" she said in broken Tigrigna.

Aisha felt slighted. *How dare she*, was what first came to her mind, but she held her tongue. She tried to reason with her young listener: "I was as brash an idealist as you once, but know this: it takes time to build a nation. It took many atrocious wars waged over many centuries for the West to get to where it is now. We're not perfect, I admit, but we're learning from our mistakes. We will find a way."

"The dream has been defiled," an older caller said. "We can't shut our eyes and ears anymore. We can't let the wound fester. It will kill us." Aisha found it reprehensible that her fellow Eritreans expressed their opposition to their leaders in such a public way, but she couldn't admonish them on air. She started to dread these calls. She wished she had a way of filtering them out.

"Instead of placating your listeners with platitudes you don't believe in yourself, you could use your platform for good," another caller said. "Why don't you join forces with those of us working to fix things? What are you afraid of?"

This last question struck a chord. Was she afraid of something? Then one day, on her ride home from the radio station, she found herself reimagining the program's function. She started mentally composing her next piece — something about the need to revisit the tenets of the rebellion that birthed their nation and the real risk of perpetuating the crimes of the oppressor. She was still aware of a transgression taking place, but the possibility of being part of something meaningful again had created an exhilarating sense of purpose in her. But soon after that, the Ethiopian invasion was announced, and she and most of her listeners closed rank around the Eritrean government, rallying back against the common enemy.

"Maybe you can work in communications, then, in that war of yours," Adam says. "If you must go, I'd rather you stay as far from the front lines as possible."

"Yes, maybe."

They smoke in silence for a while.

"Well, we better get going if we want to make it to the airport on time," Adam says.

Aisha nods without looking at him, aware of the tension of goodbyes building up between them.

Adam turns the CD player on. Mulatu Astatke's smooth "Tizita" fills the car like a soft, fragrant perfume. He then switches the dial to the radio.

"Why?" Aisha asks, looking at him with a frown.

"Too sad."

The slow lament of the saxophone in "Tizita" has become Aisha's earworm. A piece that, without words, articulates all the ways she loves Adam: the way he finds her when she loses herself in the turbid waters of blind restlessness, the way he holds her gaze with lustful eyes as he eagerly peels her clothes off, the way he sometimes makes her want to bask in the dreams afforded normal couples. She looks out the window. The sun has spread its red hue on the horizon like a wildfire about to consume the black trees in its path. The apartment buildings loom over the silhouettes of teenagers on the basketball court.

She smiles. Before she met Adam, sunsets were only the end of a long day. The subtleties of colour in a sunny sky didn't mean anything but favourable weather to her. She imagines how he would describe the horizon she's looking at: "Like an abstract painting of energetic brushstrokes of black ink on a crimson background. There is a fiery energy in the way the landscape is resisting its descent into darkness."

Adam suddenly stops the car a few metres from the turn onto Main Street and pushes the hazard lights on.

"Don't leave, Aisha. It's not too late to change your mind," he says, his voice firm.

She looks into his eyes for a second and turns her head away, aware of the doubt filling her own eyes.

"I'm not my country, Aisha. And you're not yours," he continues.

When she first started dating Adam, her friend Semra had told her, "I know you're scared, but holding his background like a noose around his neck is not the way."

Before she met Adam, Aisha could always tell right from wrong. Now she wishes that, if only for a moment, she could glimpse the future, see all the complications, hurt, and beauty that are overwhelming her senses detangled and clearly laid out. But it doesn't work like that. She turns and examines Adam again: his thick facial hair so black, almost blue in the twilight; his big melancholic eyes surrounded by deep creases; his smoke-stained full lips; his skin just light enough to give in to blushing; his hooked nose she enjoyed teasing him about. She remembers something else Adam said. Something she'd almost forgotten she'd heard: "I've lost people to Mengistu's regime too, Aisha. We've both lost people."

She leans her head back and takes in these words again.

She then lets herself open up to other thoughts. She thinks about her old frustration with the Eritrean government that, many years ago, had denied her and many of her female comrades their dues — the disillusionment that had pushed her to seek asylum in Canada. She thinks about the conservative society of her upbringing that might threaten the freedoms she's come to take for granted in her new home. She allows herself to reconsider using the radio program to speak up about women's and girls' rights and to hold the Eritrean government accountable, not only for its past shortcomings, but also for those that will inevitably arise from this new war. Would speaking up now amount to treachery? Will there ever be a right time?

She extends her hand and gently covers Adam's fist around the gear shift knob. She offers him a light smile, almost too afraid to give in to a real one.

They sit still for a long time while darkness finishes swallowing their day and the sun begins to loom on the other side of the world.

LATER, AISHA REALIZES that Ethiopia's new attack on Eritrea's sovereignty was only part of what made her want to return home. She remembers a lonely and taciturn old Somali man she met at the hospital where she worked. The old man's landlord had found him on the floor of his apartment, lying in his own excrement, after he'd suffered a severe stroke that left him paralyzed from the neck down. A nurse had told Aisha about the old man, thinking she might be Somali too. Aisha had heard of these kinds of things before. Lonely immigrants, usually older and male, whose decomposing bodies are often discovered in sparsely furnished apartments by landlords or neighbours disturbed by the smell. But this particular tragedy happened a few days after the news of Ethiopia's invasion of Eritrea had reached her. That day, as she stared at the old man's bony face, a fear she'd never known gripped her soul. She pictured all those immigrants who'd let the decades-old dream at the centre of all their dreams—the inevitability of their glorious return home—slip away with their last breath, acutely aware of their failure. She knew Adam would deem her fear irrational, but that's when a conviction as hard as a rock started to form in her heart. She didn't want to die alone on foreign soil. If she had to die, she wanted to die among her own people and for a cause worth dying for. She wanted to be buried in the Semhar of her birth, the smell of warm sea breeze in her nostrils and the taste of salt on her tongue.

spilled water

"HALLOWEEN IS A CANADIAN HOLIDAY," CLAIRE, my adoptive mother, said as she drove me and my new brother, Josh, to the mall a week before Halloween. I didn't want to sit in the back with Josh but I was ten years old so I couldn't sit in the front yet. Noticing my perplexed look in the rear-view mirror, she translated: "It's *amet baal*. We put costumes on and go around the neighbourhood and people give children candies."

"Like *Enkutatash*," I said. "In Addis Ababa, girls go around the neighbourhood, singing, and people give money. Boys make pictures of saints and sell them." I didn't know what *costume* meant but I was too excited by the prospect of celebrating a familiar holiday to bother asking. Besides, going to the mall had, in the past two months since I'd moved into my new life, meant only one thing: shopping. And shopping was a confirmation of the life of abundance that Etagegn, the cook at the orphanage in Addis Ababa, had predicted my future would hold, and maybe even proof that, unlike the American couple I'd heard about at the orphanage, my new parents were not murderers. Surely, people didn't spend so much money on someone they planned to hurt.

About six months before my adoption was finalized, I'd overheard Nurse Meron tell Etagegn about an American man who'd killed the girl he and his wife had adopted from Ethiopia. My friend Amsalu and I had just come back from school and were hiding outside, behind the orphanage kitchen at the end of the service quarters, to avoid having to help the younger children wash up before dinner. We were crouched behind a pile of truck tires under the open kitchen window when we heard Nurse Meron and Etagegn's conversation.

"It was on the news," Nurse Meron said. "He beat her, then locked her out of his house. The girl froze to death in his backyard while he and his wife watched TV with their biological children inside."

"I never thought *ferenjoch* could hurt children," Etagegn said. "Poor girl."

"We all know kids need discipline," Nurse Meron said, "but these white people say we shouldn't spank our children from one side of their mouth and then do things to kids that shouldn't be done to adults. We shouldn't allow them to adopt our children."

The aroma of frying onions and stewing *berbere* from the kitchen was making me hungry. I pushed my hands on my belly to quiet the growl and stretched my neck closer to the window.

"*Men yedereg, dihinet*," Etagegn said, kissing her teeth.

"I'd rather stay poor. Tell me, what kind of a future is this if you end up dead or, at best, an outsider to your own language and roots?" Nurse Meron said.

"Shhh, keep your voice down. The children."

"I'm just saying..."

"Well, it's terrible, but what can be done?"

"These kids get called *nigger* at school. They're told to go back to their country."

"What's *nigger*?"

"*Baria*."

There was silence for a moment.

"Even our kids can be cruel sometimes."

"I'd rather be mistreated in my own country, by my own people."

"*Meroniye*, you're an educated woman so you understand the ways of foreigners better than I do," Etagegn said. "But you're young and never had to want for much, so you're also prone to idealism. Think about it. What's the alternative? Once they turn eighteen, it's the streets for most of these kids. All you and I can do is take care of them the best we can while they're here and pray they find good homes."

A few weeks after I heard Etagegn and Nurse Meron's exchange, I had a dream. In this dream, the woman in charge of washing the children's clothes had sent me to fetch water from the fountain behind the orphanage's service quarters. I was walking with my eyes on the narrow, uneven pathway between the kitchen and the compound wall, carrying the heavy bucket, the other arm stretched out for balance, when a man bumped into me. The bucket of water fell out of my grip and onto its side, the water spilling into the gutter and out of the compound's walls. I couldn't see the man's face because the sun was in my eyes. I stared at the empty bucket and the wet spot on the ground, my feet pinned in place, more terrified of this silent man with a shadow for a face than of Mrs. Saunders, the orphanage director, who would scold me when she found out I had wasted water. I waited for the man to walk past me or say something but he just stood there blocking my way.

"*Ehil wehash alqual*," Etagegn had said with an air of mystery to her voice when I told her about my dream. "You are the water you spilled," she explained, patting my unruly hair down into a ponytail. "You're leaving the orphanage soon."

"What about the scary man?"

"He represents your destiny. The future can be frightening, but you have a bright life ahead of you. Embrace it, Nebiyat."

I was not convinced. I'd sensed something destructive in that man's presence. Or was that figure even human? I couldn't tell for sure anymore. Whatever it was, I'd felt as if it could swallow the sun and turn it into fire and ash.

Etagegn sensed my skepticism. "You're going to a much better place, Nebiyat. You'll see. I heard *ferenjoch* have so much money they even buy toys and beds for their pets. *Gwood eko new!* Can you believe that?" Just before turning to tend to her herb garden, she added, "I'm telling you, in America, even animals live better than some of us here."

Until the day I left the orphanage, I ached to tell Nurse Meron that I'd overheard her conversation with Etagegn but I didn't because she could not have prevented my adoption. And besides, everybody knew a lot of money and effort went into finding a forever family for us children, especially the older ones like me who had been waiting for years. If Mrs. Saunders had gotten wind that I didn't want to be adopted anymore, both Nurse Meron and I would have ended up in serious trouble. So to fight the fear that was growing in my chest, I started basking in Etagegn's interpretation of my dream, feeding her imagining of my future with increasingly luxurious images I collected from foreign sitcoms, movies, and magazines.

IN CONTRAST TO the Sears store where Claire had taken me three weeks earlier to get winter clothes and boots, the store we walked into was narrow and dark. Pictures of contorted, bloody faces covered the walls. The fake spiders and skeletons hanging from the ceiling reminded me of the chandeliers I had once seen at a church in Addis Ababa. I crossed myself before following Claire and Josh deeper into the store.

"I want to be a scarecrow," Josh said, picking up a package with a picture of a boy wearing a flimsy hat and tattered overalls that seemed to have been fashioned out of a potato sack and straws.

Even though he was two years younger than me, Josh and I were the same height. Noting his immaturity usually spawned in me a deep, perverse satisfaction that made his height advantage easier to bear. But now, his choice in *costume* made me think he might also not be right in the head.

"You sure?" Claire asked, examining the package.

Josh nodded.

"Once we pay for it, you can't change your mind, okay, Josh?" she said and put the package in her plastic basket.

I wondered why Claire and Paul, my adoptive father, indulged their son so much.

"Mommy, can we go to McDonald's now?" Josh asked.

We walked past shiny clothes, brightly coloured

wigs and hats, and plastic swords and guns packed on racks and shelves taller than Claire.

"Later," Claire said.

"How about you, Nebiyat? Do you want a princess costume?" she asked, placing a plastic package in front of me and pointing at a picture of a girl with blond, curly hair and a shimmering gold-and-pink puffy dress.

Before I had time to respond, she picked up another plastic-wrapped costume and asked with a big smile, "How about a butterfly?"

From the photo on the package, another girl with light brown hair as straight as Claire's, a yellow dress, and matching wings and antennae with pink spots on them smiled at me.

When Emaye, my mother, was still alive, she never asked for my opinion. When she could afford to buy me new outfits, she would always pick dark colours because light-coloured clothes stained easily and required a lot of soap to wash. She mostly wore browns or indigo herself, except for the one *habesha kemis* she kept for special occasions and one traditional white shawl with a black edge reserved for funerals and visits to the bereaved. So when Claire first asked me if I wanted the light blue sweater, white shirt, and pink skirt ensemble she'd picked up from one of the racks at Sears, I thought it was a trick question.

"It's so much more fun to shop for a girl," she'd said excitedly, as if she were buying the clothes for herself.

I'd found her enthusiasm puzzling for an adult, but it also made me feel sorry for her. I promised myself I would do my best to fill the role of a good daughter for her.

"Mommy, please?" Josh said, pulling on her sleeve.

"Soon," she said.

"But I'm hungry," Josh said, pouting.

"In a minute," she said. "Let's help your sister pick a costume first."

"This one?" I asked, pointing at the butterfly girl.

There was approval and excitement in Claire's eyes. I sighed in relief.

"No. I want to go now. And she's not my sister." Josh stomped away from her.

"Josh, don't say that," she said and went after her son. "Josh, honey, please . . ." I heard her call as she turned down an aisle.

I imagined Josh being unreasonable or acting up in front of Emaye. Emaye sometimes even hit me for looking at her the wrong way, let alone talking back. I didn't always understand what differentiated the wrong way from the right way so, for a time, I couldn't prevent myself from repeating my mistake. But eventually I figured all mothers were unpredictable and learned it was best to stare at my own feet and acquiesce even if I didn't agree.

As we left the store, I crossed myself again at a poster of a sneering old woman in black clothes and a big, pointy hat.

ONE OF MY earliest memories is of kneeling with my
parents in front of a wooden cross in our one-room
house for our nightly prayers. This was back in Addis
Ababa when I was about five years old. Sometimes my
father didn't come home after work.

"He must have lost his way home again," Emaye
would say when I asked.

I used to think it was because of his crossed eye,
which often made it seem that he was looking at two
things at once. I felt sorry for him, but Emaye would
curse at him in the mornings as she yanked my arms
through my school uniform shirt sleeves and polished
my face clean with Vaseline and spit. When I came back
from school, I'd find her still cursing, this time under
her breath, a flow of incomprehensible words accom-
panying her every step and gesture as she went about
her daily chores. Sometimes she'd stop pounding on
the rich neighbours' clothes she washed for money in
a large tub propped up on a pile of big truck tires and
lament with foamy palms open to the sky: "What did
I do to deserve this, *Amlaké*? What did I do?"

After she became too ill to kneel down — long
after my father had left us for good and long after
she'd stopped going out at night, her mouth painted
red like a fresh wound — Emaye would lie still on the
sagging bed she and I shared and guide my prayers.
She looked as though she were sinking farther and farther into the mattress every day, the sheets and *gabi*

covering her body growing, it seemed, thicker and thicker. Sometimes spit flew out of her mouth when she coughed. To avoid looking at her gaunt face and withered limbs, I'd watch the spit's trajectory as it drew an arc in the air and imagine it transformed into a fly. Or, with my head on the mattress, I'd play with slivers of straw from our broom and the bread or *injera* crumbs I'd find under the bed. Then one day Emaye's friend barred me from entering our house and, sniffling under her *netela*, said: "Your mother is no longer of this world." I thought the bed must have finished swallowing Emaye whole. I assumed that my father would come back for me but he never did.

TWO DAYS BEFORE HALLOWEEN, I watched as Claire carved two eyes and a mouth in each of the two pumpkins we'd bought at the grocery store. She then collected the flesh and seeds she'd carved out and tossed everything in the bin for *compost*, which I understood to be another word for *garbage*. I had seen my new parents throw out leftover food, and put perfectly good bottles and jars in a blue bin for a person called *recycling*. Emaye or the women at the orphanage would have reused those jars for years. It baffled me, the carelessness with which my new parents rid themselves of things. It made me wonder if I could also be discarded as easily.

"Why you put this there?" I ventured, pointing at

the candles Claire placed in the hollow space inside the pumpkins, trying to roll my *r* the way my new family did. Unlike the English I'd practised with Nurse Meron at the orphanage and at school in Addis Ababa, my new family's English sounded like a voice on a fast-forwarding tape recorder. Sometimes I asked questions just to make sure I could still speak. What if, one day, I lost my voice completely from lack of practice? Other times, I worried my new parents might think me too curious, so I dumped my questions in a pile of all the things that were incomprehensible to me.

"It's tradition," Claire said as she placed the pumpkins on each side of the doorsteps. "And it's fun. You see?" She pointed at the candlelight.

It didn't look like fun to me. The light transformed the pumpkins into two decapitated fat men, grinning threateningly. It also reminded me of what Emaye had told me about devil worshippers who left food under trees for pagan gods or those who would lace leftovers with witchcraft and throw them on the doorsteps of the people they wanted to hurt. I wondered if *ferenjoch* performed witchcraft too.

While I was at the orphanage, one of my friends had said that my new family would turn me into a Muslim. She'd crossed herself three times as she said this, her distress fully displayed in her big, protruding eyes.

"No, *ferenjoch* are Catholics, you idiot," Yohannes, another kid, had said to her. Yohannes was holding onto the street light pole outside the orphanage and swinging his body in semi-circles. "Catholic, that's what you'll become," he'd said, turning to me with a smirk that implied, *This is what you signed up for. Get used to it.*

I didn't know anything about Catholics but I figured they were probably as bad as Muslims. I wished I could tell Yohannes I would refuse to go live with such people, but we all knew none of us children had any say in these matters. I looked to Amsalu for support. She was two years older than us and always reading, so I'd hoped she'd refute Yohannes's declaration, but she kept her myopic eyes on her sweater, picking lint off her sleeves as if she were ridding her clothes of lice.

"Nobody is going to make me do anything. I'll stay a true Christian, an Orthodox Christian, until I die," I said to Yohannes, as Emaye had taught me to respond to blasphemers, and quickly walked away before any of my friends had a chance to provide more proof of my impending doom.

"They'll feed you pig meat!" I heard Yohannes shout behind me.

"What does pig meat look like?" I asked Etagegn in the evening.

Etagegn had a puzzled look for a moment before she conceded: "I don't know. But the bible says 'It's not what goes in your mouth that defiles you but what comes out of it,' so just eat whatever they give you, *eshi?*"

Later on, I realized I should have pointed out to my friends that we all shared the same fate. Who else did they hope would adopt them but *ferenjoch*? They're the only ones with too much money and no children of their own, but by the time I thought of it, I was already on the plane, on my way to Canada.

For weeks after I'd moved into my new life, I looked with fearful anticipation for signs of Catholic rituals in everything my new family did. I tried to read in their words hints of my upcoming conversion, but there was never any mention of it. In fact, I started to think maybe this family didn't believe in any god at all and wondered which was worse: being Catholic or living like animals, as Emaye would have said, without any faith.

THE DAY BEFORE HALLOWEEN, I was helping Paul and Josh carry paper bags full of dry leaves and twigs to the edge of the sidewalk for the compost truck to pick up, when I heard Josh shout: "I found a worm." It was getting dark so I couldn't see what he was holding between his fingers, but there was an excitement in his voice as though he'd found gold. I dropped the bag I was carrying and ran to see this thing called *worm*.

"It's a big one," Josh said, turning toward me and dangling the worm in front of me, almost touching my nose with it.

I let out a small scream and walked away in disgust.

Josh followed me with excitement in his voice. "You're such a baby. Who's scared of worms?" He laughed and chased me around the yard.

"No, Josh. It's dirty, stop it," I said. "Stop it!" I shrieked and turned to slap his hand away but ended up hitting him hard on the face.

He stumbled backwards and fell, the worm flying out of his hand and landing behind him.

"Nebiyat!" Paul shouted, dropping his rake and taking big steps toward us.

"She hit me," Josh cried. "Nebiyat hit me."

I pointed at the ground. Paul followed my trembling finger then looked back up at me and asked, "What happened?"

"What did I tell you, Nebiyat? We don't hit," Claire said, standing beside Paul and Josh, the three of them forming a semicircle in front of me. "This," she continued, grabbing my hand and gently slapping it, "not okay."

I bobbed my head. "I'm sorry. I'm sorry," I stuttered, my heart about to jump out of my throat, beating as if it didn't want to belong to my body anymore.

Paul and Claire exchanged a look I'd come to hate and dread. As I walked into the house and to my room, I felt as though a thousand horror-filled eyes were following me. This was the way I'd been feeling at school since, two weeks earlier, I'd twisted one of my classmate's fingers for laughing and pointing at me while saying things I didn't quite understand about Africa and

food. Eyes and whispers had been trailing me through
lunch queues at the cafeteria and even when I hid in
bathroom stalls at recess.

I took my shoes off in the entranceway and walked
past a wall of pictures of Paul, Claire, Josh, and other
people who resembled one another. I stopped for a
moment to look at a picture taken a month and half
earlier. In this photograph, I'm sitting on the grass
beside Josh in the backyard and Paul, Claire, and their
parents are crouched around us. The day it was taken,
Paul and Claire had invited their friends and families
to meet me.

"Nice to meetchya, Nebiyat. Did I get it right? Ne-bi-
yat? What a pretty girl," the guests had said, looking at
Claire and Paul as if I were a great treasure find.

"How interesting," they said when Claire translated
what my name meant. "Prophetess, huh? It's not something you hear often around here. Well done."

Some of them had concern in their eyes that con-
tradicted their smiles and words, a look that reminded
me of the way Emaye's friends treated me when they
learned I was being sent to an orphanage. I nodded,
smiled, and thanked my new parents' guests, trying
to pin odd-sounding names to unfamiliar features.
Examining the picture again, my dark face like a
bruise in the midst of sunny smiles and my hair a big
pile of coiled yarn sitting in the middle of my head
after Claire had broken her fine-toothed comb trying

to detangle my tight curls, I felt like an aberration. A rough and awkward snag on a tapestry of seamless and easy belonging.

Claire came to sit beside me on my bed and put her hand on mine. I flinched but didn't remove my hand. I was still shaken by the sight of the worm, which brought to mind those that slid out of me when I squatted in the latrine when I was little. The intricate veins on the back of Claire's hand were green and clearly visible. I imagined a tree was growing inside her. It reminded me of one of Mrs. Saunders's stories about carnivorous trees that preyed on small children who refused to go to sleep.

My eyes filled up with tears.

"Maybe we should find someone who speaks Amharic," Claire said, patting my hand and turning to Paul who was standing by the door.

I looked at Claire's eyes, which were brownish-green like water-starved grass. "Your new mother has the eyes of a cat. Maybe she turns into one at night," Yohannes had teased me while I was still at the orphanage. I wondered if having cat eyes was a sign of a murderous soul.

"We've discussed this already. Full immersion is best in the long term. Speaking Amharic will only slow down her progress in English. And her integration," Paul said. "It's normal for kids to fight. We'll figure it out. Right, Nebiyat?" he continued, now on his knees in front of my bed. There was something in his gaze that contrasted with his reassuring voice. I couldn't tell if it was exasperation or worry.

The light gleamed on the wisps of blond facial hair that grew on his chin and along his jawline. The corners of his eyes creased in an arc when he smiled but his droopy blue eyes made him look sad, as if he carried the weight of the sky in them. When I first met him at the orphanage, I thought I could find comfort and kinship in the sorrow of his eyes. Now I wondered if Paul was, as Emaye used to describe deceitful people, a false prophet in disguise.

"Do as you're told until you're old enough to take care of yourself, but don't trust anyone, *eshi*?" Nurse Meron had said. Remembering Nurse Meron's words made me feel heavy with defeat. I had known from the beginning that, as an outsider, a lot would be riding on my behaviour, that I needed to stay vigilant, but it seemed I was bound to fail at every turn.

I wanted to disappear. I wanted to be sent back home where adults said exactly what they meant and where I knew what was expected of me.

I looked around my room, remembering how excited I'd been the first time I laid eyes on it. How cautiously I'd sat on my bed beside Claire as she unpacked my luggage, worried that the furniture might reject my body. How, as I discreetly slid my feet back and forth on the soft, brownish-yellow carpet with piles that made my bedroom floor look like a field of wheat grains, my eyes darting from the sunflowers of the thick comforter on the bed to the matching lamp, then to the painting of foaming sea waves on the wall, I'd wished that my friends from the orphanage were there to see what I was seeing. To touch what I was touching. A whole room to myself. No bunk beds that creaked like old people's knees, no unstable dressers that threatened to collapse on you every time you opened a drawer. No cold cement floors and no holes, cracks, or stains of little dirty hands on the walls.

"Smile. Even when you have nothing to smile about," Nurse Meron had told me before I'd left the orphanage. "And don't forget to say *thank you*, *sorry*, and *please*. You do these things and you'll be okay," she'd said, a cloud of concern in her eyes.

But that first night, as I looked around my room, I didn't have to pretend. I was genuinely grateful to Claire and Paul.

After my new parents left, I sat on my bed with my legs folded in front of me for a while, chewing on my nails until I drew blood. Then I kneeled down with my elbows propped on my bed and prayed. I thanked Emaye, and Jesus, Mary, and God, and all the saints my mother now lived with for having looked over me until this point. I prayed for the soul of that poor girl who was killed in America and for God to give me the strength, patience, and understanding to behave as my new parents required me to until I was old enough to take care of myself.

That night, after Josh frightened me with the worm, I dreamed I was a butterfly. I followed other butterflies higher and higher into the sky and farther and farther away from my new home. The other butterflies were as colourful as I was, and their faces were those of my friends from the orphanage. I could feel the wind in my undone hair, which was as soft and as light as Claire's. The houses, cars, and parks below were small. I could see the orphanage, its name above the entrance gate. Farther up the road, I saw the house where I used to live with Emaye. Somehow I knew my parents were there, their eyes to the sky, waiting for me. But before I could spot them, out of nowhere, ominous grey clouds started to close in on me from all sides. My friends were quickly disappearing in the distance, and in the swelling clouds appeared the laughing faces of the children who taunted me at school. I screamed for help but no sound made it past my throat. I was alone, mute, and being tossed around by the strong wind, twirling out of control toward the ground. Right before I hit the ground, I felt someone shaking me by the shoulder. I opened my eyes and saw Claire sitting on the edge of my bed.

ON HALLOWEEN DAY, after dinner, Claire drew dots on my cheeks and nose with makeup that matched the colours of my butterfly costume. Josh came out of his room wearing his raggedy-looking costume. I inspected my reflection in the hallway mirror. The dress was pretty and the wings were so light they fluttered when I moved. I thought about all the things Claire and Paul had bought me and how they had been smiling at me, touching me, and holding my hand with a carefulness that made me think of Mrs. Saunders's expensive glass vases. Was I wrong to fear them? To question their intentions? Despite everything, Halloween might turn out to be even better than *Enkutatash*, I told myself.

"Don't you look pretty," Paul said to me, trying to adjust my antennae to fit straight on the braids I'd plaited myself the day before.

I backed away. "I will do it," I said.

"Okay. Now both of you sit down and watch TV while your mom and I put our costumes on," Paul said.

"Hurry up, Daddy," Josh said and sat on the floor in front of the TV.

After a few tries, I decided my antennae would sit better on my head if my hair was slicked back into a ponytail, so I went to ask Claire for permission to undo my braids as I was taught to do at the orphanage.

I knocked on Claire and Paul's bedroom door.

For a moment, I was aware of only my body freezing in place at the same time as my heart sank into my stomach. I couldn't lift my legs off the floor or my eyes off the creature towering over me with a dagger in its hand. I let out a shrill scream and ran toward the front door.

"Don't kill me! Don't kill me!" I cried.

"Wait...What?" I heard Paul's voice behind me.

The creature caught up with me and grabbed my arm before I could reach the door.

"Paul, wait. I think...," Claire said.

"Please don't kill me. Please," I cried, my eyes fixed on the ground, too petrified to look up.

"Your costume," Claire said.

I pulled and twisted my body to free my arm.

The creature let go of me and I fell to the ground, my knees hitting the wooden floors. The image of the chalk-white face, the bloody mouth, the protruding blood-soaked fangs, and the red-and-black cape raced across my eyes as if I were looking at the creature's reflection in a cracked mirror. The truth of what I had just seen took over me like a flow of insects, instantly spreading to every corner of my mind and body. It was Satan. I clasped my hands under my chin and curled my body into a ball. With my eyes shut tight, I recited the Lord's Prayer: *"Abatachin hoy, besemay yemitinor..."* The creature didn't look like the Satan on the picture in the prayer room at the orphanage, the one with Archangel Michael pressing down on its head. But what else could it be?

I peeked from one eye. The creature was still standing in front of me, barring my way. I felt another shiver run down my spine. I shut my eyes harder and bent my head down, my forehead almost touching the ground. I remembered the man from the dream I had at the orphanage, the one Etagegn had interpreted as a good omen. That man took on the face of the creature I'd just seen. Then I thought about the equally faceless American man who'd killed his adopted daughter.

I rocked my body as I prayed louder and louder, combating my thoughts with sound: *"Simih yikedes, mengistih timta..."*

"Paul, go change," I heard Claire say.

"Fikadih besemay endehonetch..."

"She peed. Nebiyat peed herself," Josh said.

I felt the wetness down my legs and feet.

"Shush, Josh," Paul said.

"When are we going trick-or-treating?" Josh said.

"Actually, Paul, take Josh. I'll take care of Nebiyat," Claire said.

"What I don't understand is...she's ten," Paul said. "Why would she think we're trying to kill her?"

"How would I know, Paul?" Claire's voice rose. "Please, just take Josh," she sighed.

"Maybe you're right. This is too much. We should seek help."

"Yeah..."

"Daddy," Josh said.

"We'll talk later...just go."

"I'm sorry, Nebiyat. I didn't mean to frighten you," I heard Paul say, then a cold breeze grazed my naked arms before the front door closed.

"SATAN IS A SHAPESHIFTER. He can manifest himself in any form and anywhere," Emaye used to say. "You have to pray to the Lord Jesus Christ. He's your only shield against the Devil." When I was little, I used to be scared to sleep by myself or go to the outhouse alone at night, imagining Satan waiting for me in the dark, in the middle of a great fire, ready to pounce on me, his eyes, horns, and limbs all red and black at the edges, where the fire licked them. I'd also seen Satan make people speak in tongues and contort their bodies like animals fighting slaughter at the Pentecostal church Emaye took me to once when she got mad at some people at her own church. Sometimes, instead of attacking your body, the Devil infected your soul. But Emaye knew how to ward off evil of all sorts. She knew all the right prayers; she had special ointments and medicine her *Abba* — priest — gave her for when Satan made my belly ache, and protective inscriptions bound in a leather pouch to tie around my neck against evil eye and all otherworldly dangers. I touched my naked neck. I didn't even have a black thread, the strict minimal symbol of my Christian faith, to protect me. That's when the permanence of Emaye's death really hit me. I felt a rupture, a gaping bottomless hole where the certainty of her love and protection lived. I was really alone in the world, forsaken.

After Claire helped me clean up, I told her I wanted to go to bed. While she was busy doling out candies to trick-or-treaters, I picked up the winter jacket and boots she'd bought me, and jumped out of my bedroom window and into the cold night.

TWO DECADES LATER, after a year of researching my father's whereabouts, I bought a ticket to Addis Ababa to meet him. On my flight there, I had a thousand questions running through my head, but as my father and I sat on short stools forming a triangle with our translator, all the things I wanted to ask seemed too trivial or too personal to voice in front of a stranger. We sat together, tongue-tied but full of the sorrow of a broken history. We smiled and searched in each other's faces for a thread to sew that history back together. To need a middleman into the heart of the person who gave me life, to require a roadmap into a culture and language that were mine at birth, stung at first. It then turned into a grudge that I kept hidden in a far corner of my consciousness.

"It's good you're not all alone over there. You have your daughters," my father said through our translator, a picture of my family in his hands.

It suddenly dawned on me that Emaye might have disapproved of my association with the man who'd abandoned us so many years earlier.

"You have a big family. That's nice," I said, examining the faces of half-siblings and cousins from my father's side assembled around us, wondering if our translator could convey the bitterness in my voice.

"I'm glad you kept your name. Your mother picked it," my father said, taking my hand in his.

I looked at our intertwined fingers, the seamless transition between his skin tone and mine, as though our hands were two different parts of the same body.

"Yes, I kept my name," I replied, as if I'd had any say in the matter. Then I repeated those words to myself, slowly letting this new knowledge, the root of my name, wash over me and atone for the years I'd wished, growing up in Canada, for a less conspicuous name, for a name that didn't encourage the unwarranted curiosity and inevitable pity of transracial adoption stories, a name free of the shame and anger of unbelonging.

On Emaye's side of the family, I noticed my cousin's crooked pinky, an exaggerated version of my own. I thought I recognized Emaye's smile in a distant aunt's and her scolding words in another's tone. I wanted to tell them it took me a long time to forgive Emaye for having deserted me. Even longer to let scar tissue take hold in the cold, hollow space inside where I'd stored my loss. But language failed me.

Going through pictures of my Canadian family with my newly found relatives, and later on, lying by myself in a hotel room with city smells and rhythms now foreign to me, I missed the ease with which I moved in that other world, the love of that other family anxiously waiting for me in Canada. I realized then that home and belonging would never be clear-cut notions for me. Like my father's wandering eye, my heart and mind will always be vacillating between two possibilities, eyeing two realities at the same time. And I felt something like an acceptance, a new way of being in the world.

But on that Halloween night back in Canada, all those years earlier, as I walked farther and farther away from my adoptive parents' house, cupping my ears against the needling pain of cold, I wasn't thinking about my name or where I belonged. I was mourning Emaye's passing, crying for the safety of her arms, the soothing feel of her fingers as she traced lines on my scalp with paraffin oil, the comfort of her laughter and the sound of her voice as she hummed songs of her own childhood to me. I was crying for that nameless girl who froze to death in America. I imagined her banging on the door to the backyard, screaming and crying until her hands hurt and her voice became hoarse, then curling up in a corner in despair. How lonely she must have felt, abandoned by those who'd promised to care for her, and so far away from all she'd ever known.

The clouds of sadness and apprehension lifted only early the next day when, still fearful for my life and full of the pain of loss, I arrived home, accompanied by police officers who'd found me coiled on a park bench about ten blocks away. It wasn't in Paul's worried eyes, as he waited barefoot on the front lawn, a phone to his ear, or in Claire's cries as she stood beside him looking haggard in her bathrobe and dishevelled hair, that I finally found solace. What opened up the possibility of a new sense of kinship, what made me feel that I mattered to someone again, was when Josh ran up to me and hugged me hard, almost making me lose my balance.

not a small thing

WHEN I HEARD ABOUT WHAT HAPPENED TO YOU, Mark and I were at Elaine's place. We had just ordered from Pizza Hut on Yonge Street, and Elaine was trying to explain to Mark why men shouldn't use the word *bitch*, ever, regardless of who they were referring to or why, the same way *nigger* should always be off limits for non-black people. And predictably, Mark was arguing it was not the same thing. Your mom called me.

After I hung up with her, I blurted out, "Selam was attacked." I was just repeating your mom's words. I hadn't yet grasped their full meaning.

"What? Attacked how?" Elaine asked, grabbing me by the arm.

"They pulled her by her hijab. She fell..."

"Is she okay?" Elaine said.

"Who are *they*?" Mark asked.

"I don't know. Some guys," I said.

Elaine and I reached for our cellphones.

We called you, texted you, tried to reach you on Twitter to no avail.

"Did someone intervene at least?" Mark asked.

I shook my head. I couldn't feel my body against the wooden chair. I stared at my phone.

"Did she go to the police?" Elaine asked.

I thought about our last time together. Our fight. I felt as though I had something to do with the attack, as if I'd sent those guys to hurt you.

"Yeah," I said, my voice cracking a little.

The doorbell rang and Mark got up to answer it.

D'Angelo's "The Charade" played lightly on Elaine's laptop. I thought of how you, Elaine, and I were taken by *Black Messiah* two years earlier. We were too young to appreciate D'Angelo's artistry when his earlier albums were released, but *Black Messiah* was of our time. It spoke to us.

"Is there something we can do?" Mark said.

I shrugged.

We all stared at the unopened box of pizza Mark had placed on the table. The smell made me feel a little nauseated.

"To think this kind of shit can happen here," Mark said.

We were all silent for a while.

"What's crazy is that what's happening to Muslim women here these days is what happened in Iran in the eighties, in places like Algeria in the nineties and, more recently, in Egypt but in reverse," Elaine said.

"Why do people care so much about what others wear?" Mark said.

"The same misogyny that makes you, a Black man, think you're entitled to use words that are demeaning to women," Elaine said.

I wished I was alone. I didn't want your ordeal to be on display as if you were an anonymous victim of a hate crime we were discussing in one of our political science or criminology classes. I knew how much this kind of exposure would hurt you.

"Elaine, you can't be serious?" Mark said.

"It stems from the same urge to control women," Elaine said. "In Algeria, women's uncovered legs or hair were suddenly seen as a symbol of Western oppression—"

"Did the women ask the men to go back to wearing their traditional clothes too? I mean, if you're rejecting Western influence," Mark said, his lips stretching into a sarcastic smile.

"Yeah right," Elaine said. "That's what I'm trying to tell you. Turns out, the attacks were sparked by some politician or cleric blaming working women for high unemployment rates." She tucked strands of her straight weave behind her ear. "So basically, they wanted to frighten the women into staying home. Same way men here use words such as *bitch*, *slut*, or *cunt* to debase or intimidate outspoken women into silence."

I wished they would both keep quiet. I wanted to leave but my feet wouldn't move. I sat there staring at my phone. I thought about you, about all the years we'd been best friends, all the ways you'd shaped my life, and how I'd failed you when you needed me most.

WE MET IN tenth grade. You didn't wear the hijab back then. I'd transferred from another school that year. I sat beside you, not because I found you likeable, but because you were the only other Black girl—and the only *Habesha* kid—in the class. We were about the same height and complexion but that was where our resemblance ended. You had the slow, confident gait of someone who owned the ground they stood on while I waddled about with the gracelessness of a lost soul. Your clear, musical voice carried well while mine struggled to be heard even when I sat at the front of the class. I found you irritating and riveting at the same time. The way the sharp angles of your long face, which usually made you look tough, curved themselves into an astonishing softness when you smiled, as though you were sculpted from copper. The way you raved about Afrofuturism, from Samuel R. Delany to Nalo

Hopkinson, from Sun Ra to Janelle Monáe, before any of us even knew the term. It was as if you had a secret window into a higher plane of existence.

The first time we really talked, we were in the school gym with the rest of the class, hanging posters of Harriet Tubman and Viola Desmond for Black History Month.

"If you could go back in time, where would you go?" you asked me.

"I guess as a Black person, I'd say Africa before the Europeans discovered it," I said, putting *discovered* in quotation marks to impress you, "but as a woman..."

"Just like Black history didn't start with slavery or colonialism, women weren't always treated as second-class citizens. At least not in all cultures," you said. "So that this-is-as-good-as-it's-ever-gotten-for-you narrative is misleading at best."

You stopped to unfold another poster. "Take, for example, the concept of gender and sexual fluidity. In many Indigenous cultures, this was a well-understood and respected aspect of human behaviour. Until the Europeans forced their rigid biblical views on them, that is. Muslim conquerors weren't any better."

You moved and talked so fast, I needed a moment to grasp all that you'd said. "Okay... so where would you go then?" I asked.

"If I could, I'd go back to the time when Yodit Gudit ruled the Abyssinian kingdom," you said, as though it were the most obvious answer. "I'd be one of her generals or something."

I didn't know who or what you were talking about. "Oh yeah?"

"Queen Yodit gets a bad rep 'cause she burned down some churches and shit. As we know, history always sides with the winners, in this case the Ethiopian Orthodox Church, but I think she was awesome, a real trailblazer."

"That doesn't necessarily mean women had it better back in the day though, right?" I said. "Look at the U.S. and Obama. According to the Southern Poverty Law Center, there are a whole lot more white supremacist groups now than under Bush." I hoped this would make up for my ignorance of Ethiopian history.

"Well, Yodit ruled for forty years. That's almost two generations," you said.

"Still."

You weren't listening to me anymore. "Can you imagine that? Forty years of continuous female leadership? I mean, not the same woman the whole time, of course, but..." You leaned against the wall beside a large print of Rosemary Brown. You swivelled a roll of duct tape around your index finger, your eyes full of possibilities I couldn't even begin to imagine.

That's when I first fell in love with you. The first time I felt that, with you as my friend, I could become more knowledgeable, more worldly. But our friendship really took off that day when the girl who sat across from you in history class suggested you ask your parents to hire a babysitter to take care of your younger siblings so you could attend the school dance together.

"It's not your friggin' responsibility," she'd said.

I thought I read a hint of condescension in your smile as you listened to her. You had your arms folded around a binder with a picture of young Angela Davis and her glorious afro adorning its plastic cover. As soon as the girl left, you looked at me and laughed out loud, your body folding in two. I giggled uncomfortably.

"Imagine that," you said. "Asking my poor immigrant mother to hire a babysitter with the money she earns counting pennies in a freezing parking lot booth so that *I*, her teenage daughter, can attend a school dance."

I joined in, picturing my own parents' reaction to such a suggestion. And that shared laughter felt so warm and familiar, it was as if we'd laughed together many times before, in another lifetime.

"I CAN'T BELIEVE nobody intervened," Mark said, breaking my train of thought.

Elaine grabbed small plates from the kitchen cupboard. "With all the fear mongering and scapegoating politicians spew these days...Remember the barbaric cultural practices hotline?"

Mark put a slice of pizza on my plate. "True," he

said. "Problem is we do denial too well in this country."

"Reminds me of Ursula Le Guin's story 'The Ones Who Walk Away from Omelas.' Have you read it?" she asked me.

"No," I said, staring at my slice of pepperoni pizza. It lay across my plate, drenched in oil and melted cheese. It made me think of skin ulcer.

"It's about this society where the citizens' happiness depends on one child's constant suffering," Elaine said. "Everyone knows what's up but they turn a blind eye to preserve the status quo."

"Right," Mark said. "What bugs me in that story is how the few who empathize with the child choose to leave the city instead of trying to fix things."

"A lot of liberals fit that description. They talk the talk, but when shit goes down, they're MIA," Elaine said, picking at her pizza crust.

I wanted to tell them I couldn't care less about Le Guin or their opinions on the matter, but I didn't.

Frank Ocean's "Wiseman" was playing now. The sadness of the song melded with my own.

"Should we go to Selam's?" Mark asked.

I shook my head. "She won't let us see her."

I thought of the time you'd locked yourself in your room for two days after your grandmother's funeral, refusing to greet well-wishers as was expected of you. You shared your joy and outrage freely but you confronted your hurts and pains privately.

WHEN I WAS LITTLE, whenever I heard my parents talk about what they'd endured and overcome before they made it to Canada, I'd assumed that I, by reason of being their offspring, would have inherited their courage and resilience as though these were a pre-installed computer program that could be activated when necessary. But I was always afraid. Of things I could imagine — loneliness, rejection, disease, violence — and of things that existed only in dark corners of my mind, outside the realm of words or logic.

When I confessed this to you, you told me you'd read something about children inheriting their parents' trauma: "For example, children of survivors of the Holocaust who'd never faced any violence themselves showed signs of stress disorder."

It didn't matter whether this was true. I was grateful to you for giving my irrational fears legitimacy.

"But I'm too cautious for my own good sometimes," I argued, hungry for more affirmation.

"Caution is good," you said. "Heck, I could use some of that myself sometimes." You laughed.

There was this aura about you that inspired trust and confidence. You made me believe that I — the fearful, indecisive girl who'd always stuck to challenges she knew were manageable — had chosen Morpheus's red pill of my own accord. I believed in your belief in me. We became inseparable. We shared everything: books, music, idols, hairstyles, clothes. I called us twins.

You named us SPLIF: Short People Liberation Front. We rarely quarreled, but when we did, it always surprised our friends how easily we made up. Inevitably, one of us would say: "We're all that we got." And the other would reply: "And that's not a small thing."

"HEY, GIRL, CHILL," Elaine said, patting my hand. "You look like someone poisoned your food. I'm sure Selam will be fine. She's a warrior. One way or another, she'll make those men pay." She pushed my plate closer to me.

We all smiled a little.

This much I knew. There was so much willpower and righteousness beating inside you, it radiated through your words, your eyes, your skin. Even back in high school, you wouldn't allow anyone to demean you, or let hatred or willful ignorance slide. One day my neighbour, a lonely woman in her fifties, told us to go back to our country because she thought we were being too loud.

"Who the fuck do you think is going to pay for your retirement if we go? The children you didn't have?" you'd yelled at her while I stood frozen in place.

And that other time when this Asian guy asked me what the big fuss was with Angelina Jolie's adopted Black daughter's hair.

"Hair is hair, right?" he'd said, with a smug smile.

"You should've asked him if he'd tell the thousands

of Asian women going under the knife every year that eyes are just eyes," you'd said when I told you about it.

It annoyed me that you could be so quick on your feet. I said, "I told him to imagine people waving their fingers right in his face again and again, and then each time, complimenting him on his normal vision as though to say the shape of his eyes was not a defect after all."

In reality, I'd been so dumbfounded I'd just stared at the guy. There was such a confidence in his tone that it made me think that maybe I, and Black people in general, were just overreacting after all. I'd struggled to string words together to convey my thoughts before I half-heartedly mumbled something about deeply ingrained racism in the history of the United States.

But willpower alone can only sustain you for so long. As my mother always said, the world doesn't tolerate audacious girls. I tried to imagine your attacker—a teenager or a grown man?—pulling on your veil from behind while his friends hurled racist insults at you, you tripping on your long skirt as you staggered backward. I pictured the glare of naked hatred on his face, his mouth contorting, about to froth with satisfied lust. The obscenity of it all. I imagined your shock. Did you turn around and hold his stare? Did you curse at him? Or did you blink away, ashamed of what transpired between you, of your vulnerability and his power? Would looking away have erased what took place, rewound time so you could've crossed the street and avoided what happened? I pictured you on the ground, holding your hijab in your lap as though it was your soul just torn out of your body. I imagined you being surprised by how much the hijab meant to you even though you'd only been wearing it for a month. Did you cry? I hope you did, Selam, even if it was only later on, in the confines of your bedroom. Otherwise this shit will eventually tear you apart.

I GREW UP in a strict Pentecostal household. My parents' incontrovertible faith dictated the words I spoke in the house, the thoughts I thought. Their beliefs laced all my adolescent interests with sin, whether it was music, dancing — other than swaying to church songs — alcohol, cigarettes, or sex. You grew up in a non-observant Muslim family. Your mother had been a doctor back home and a women's rights activist and had only taken the hijab after she'd moved to Canada because she'd felt isolated. "The veil," you told me, "is her way of connecting with her past and of finding a community." She was your hero. I envied you. I took it for granted that you'd share my contempt for all religious dogma, but to my dismay, you were full of wonder for everything faith related: Bahá'í, Christianity, Judaism, Hinduism. For a while, all you talked about was Joseph Campbell's comparative mythology and the roots of all religions;

then it was all about Karen Armstrong and her *History of God*, then onto Irshad Manji. I started to see your insatiable curiosity about spirituality as a character flaw. Why would a girl as intelligent as you waste her time with the irrational world of religions? Your obsession even scared me sometimes.

You dismissed my budding atheism with a sweep of your hand. *"Pfff. That's wack,"* you said.

You couldn't see that you'd hurt my feelings. Back then, nothing seemed to be personal with you. "Any rational person would know that the world would be a better place without religion and the hive mentality it incites," I said.

You rolled your eyes. "Have you heard of Richard Dawkins and his followers? It's no better than a cult. A bunch of trust fund kids or white, middle-class men who are quick to dismiss POCs' and poor people's need for community, while they themselves live and work surrounded by people who look and think like them, and institutions that protect their interests and well-being."

As usual, the words tumbled out of your mouth so quickly that I only understood all that you'd said after you were gone. It took me even longer to find holes in your argument, but by then we had moved on to agnosticism.

"Also, why don't you ask your parents about the Derg's atheist government they fled from or read up on Russia's or China's state atheism?" you said.

With you, I was always behind the curve.

We'd settled on agnosticism after watching an interview with Margaret Atwood. There was something alienating and brash about this affirmation that made me feel still edgy and different enough while making me feel closer to you. This assertion also gave my resentment against my parents' blind faith an intellectual outlet. I even wrote a paper in my social sciences and humanities class in grade twelve that sealed my decision to study political science at the University of Toronto. Do you remember it? It was titled "The Pentecostal Church's Insidious Exploitation of Africa's Most Vulnerable." You chose to major in biology to follow in your mother's footsteps and become a doctor.

We were getting ready for our first frosh week party when you said, "We can't prove whether God exists or not. Heck, we might even have invented It the day our ancestors first buried their dead with their belongings, but that shouldn't be the end of the road, right?" I knew it was a rhetorical question. I should have known your restless mind couldn't settle on anything for long. But I was having too much fun to bother so I shrugged and let it slide.

Do you remember that party, Selam? How you, I, Elaine, Mark, and so many of the friends we grew up with danced and sang along to our favourite songs? We jumped along to Kendrick Lamar's "Alright," our arms around each other's backs, repeating the chorus: "We gon' be alright." Do you remember the energy, Selam? The joy? Nothing could have touched us that night. Nothing could have broken that circle. It was like the coming together of the tribe. By the end of the night, your voice was hoarse and my toes hurt from the high heels I wore, but we were beaming. We'd finally made it to university and the future was a blank page thirsty for our ink. Plus, I was about to move to my own place. I felt I could do or be anything. It was the best night of my life.

"I THINK WE should go see her," Elaine said. "Even if she doesn't want us to. We should still try."

I nodded.

"Let me get my things," Elaine said and went to her bedroom.

Mark took the box of leftover pizza and our plates to the kitchen.

I sat by the living room window and called you again. Then I tried to replay our last fight so I could understand how we ended up estranged. Once in a while, I looked at my cellphone, hoping against hope that you'd at least text me.

THE DAY YOU announced you were thinking of wearing the hijab, we were at Mark's parents' house celebrating his nineteenth birthday. You, Elaine, the guy you had a crush on, George, and I were in the backyard for some fresh air while Mark and the rest of our friends partied inside.

"I love that Erykah Badu look, Selam. It suits your face," Elaine said to you.

"I'm actually thinking of taking on the hijab," you said. "I usually find hats constraining so this is kind of a test run to see if I can handle covering my hair and ears all day long."

"Good one," I said and followed Elaine to the patio set.

"I didn't know you were Muslim," George said, sitting beside you.

I watched the light from the candles on the glass table bend and swirl in the rich brown of the rum and coke in my hand. "She's just saying that. She changes gods the way others change underwear," I said, remembering your last change of heart.

"I am a Muslim. And I *do* intend to wear the veil," you said, holding my gaze across the table.

"But you're not. I mean, religion is not a gene. It's not automatically inherited. And the hijab? Why would you do that?" I asked. Your constant ideological flip-flopping was taking its toll on me.

"Because," you said and turned to George, "Islam is

the religion my parents were raised in and I want to reconnect with that part of my heritage."

"That's the stupidest thing I've ever heard you say," I said. I shouldn't have confronted you in front of our friends, especially George, but your announcement felt like a personal affront to me, intended to spite me. "Where is this new pronouncement coming from?" I continued. I took a big gulp of my drink.

"People change. They evolve," you said to me and turned to George again. "I've always been interested in spirituality. The hijab is an external expression of my connection to the Divine."

"Whatever. Is that why you're not drinking?" I said. I leaned to the side. "And that dress," I continued, my eyes on your shapeless, long-sleeved, maxi dress.

You ignored me. "Hijab is about modesty," you said to George. "I think that's a commendable —"

"I've got news for you," I interrupted. "Wearing a hijab in a country where the majority of people don't makes you stand out. That's seeking attention, not modesty. You'll get more stares than I do in my jeans and T-shirt." The rum and coke was getting to my head. "Remember how you used to make fun of girls who cover up?"

"It's not the same thing," you said. "I made fun of *hijabis* who wore tight clothes, too much makeup and perfume. I made fun of the incongruity of their choices. But hijab when worn modestly, as intended, liberates women from men's gaze."

"Oh please, spare me," I said, taking another sip. "Why is men's lust a woman's problem anyway? Also, I'd be insulted if I were a man. Wouldn't you?" I said, turning to Elaine and George.

George cleared his throat.

"Okay. You two take it easy," Elaine said. "Can you do this another time?"

"And wasn't that you who said hijab sexualizes women as much as bikinis do?" I clawed at the table.

"Let me ask you this: When was the last time you left your room feeling at peace with your appearance? Or felt that men actually listened to what you have to say instead of—?"

"Oh, you think men are going to listen to you because you suddenly show up looking like a nun? You're delusional."

"Why are you so flustered anyway? What is it to you?" you asked.

"I don't know. Maybe it has something to do with seeing my best friend submitting herself to religious dogma and calling her newly found servitude progress," I pressed on.

You were silent for a moment, which surprised me. Somewhere inside, I knew I was revelling in the notion of, for once, being the righteous one. "For God's sake, why don't you shave your head," I said.

"Look," you said. "I haven't figured it all out yet, and I don't have to justify myself to you or to anyone else. But if I'm to be sexualized either way, at least *I* will choose my poison," you said and turned to look at George for a moment, then Elaine and me. "And besides, what's so special about your lifestyle: getting wasted daily, squandering your time and money on frivolous things, walking around half naked, auctioning yourselves to the highest bidder?"

"We all sell ourselves one way or another, honey. Don't kid yourself," Elaine said, smoothing her tight dress over her thick thighs, "whether it's our brains or bodies."

"Selam. Listen," I said. "If you're doing this to impress your mom—"

"Don't," you said, with a forcefulness that struck me silent.

I knew I was reaching. I took another sip of my drink. "Alright. Sorry, but with all that's going on in the world these days, now is really not a good time to wear a hijab."

"For some of us, being Black *and* female is challenging enough," Elaine said and got up. "I think this calls for another drink."

You sighed noisily. "When do you presume would be a good time?" you asked me.

Somewhere behind my growing irritation, a question was forming: Was your sudden interest in the veil a political stand in solidarity with practising Muslim women?

"Look," I said, "sometimes you're too impulsive for your own good but I can understand if—"

"Sometimes you're too much of a coward." Your voice was tight and cold.

Blood rushed to my head. I could smell your stubbornness, your patronizing tone. It reminded me of my parents' scorn. I wanted to crush it. Rage blurred my vision.

"Seriously, you two have to let this go," Elaine said. "Another beer, George?"

George shook his head and shifted in his seat.

Your voice softened. "Look. I'm sorry, but this is something I need to do."

I knew how to hurt you. "So how does dating work for *hijabis*?" I said, dragging my words and looking at George from the corner of my eye. "Can you still fuck or will it have to be sanctified by some old, bearded man first now? Oh, and can you date a non-Muslim, or do you only have eyes for the intense, religious types with prayer caps and flood pants?"

Your eyes shot arrows.

"Will you require a chaperone? I know someone." I couldn't stop myself.

"Okay, you two, really. Chill the fuck out. You're messing with my buzz," Elaine said and walked toward the house.

George cleared his throat again and followed her.

We could hear a reggae remix of Rihanna's "Diamonds" playing as they opened the back door to the house. A barrier of crushed expectations stood between us, blinding us to what we had been to each other. I watched the flames from the candles on the table tremble against the light summer breeze.

You picked up your purse and walked down the driveway. I sat there and watched you walk away until you disappeared around the corner. Then I watched the deserted street for a while until two guys came stumbling out of the house, laughing. One of them leaned against a tree that loomed over the dimly lit backyard like a bouquet of darkness.

"Tupac or Biggie?" I heard one of them ask, struggling to light a cigarette.

I knew what your answer to that age-old question would have been: Tupac. I smiled a small, private smile. A smile that could only have been shared with you. It made me miss the old you. Or more precisely, *my* idea of the old you. Of us.

SELAM, MY BEAUTIFUL, indomitable Selam, do you remember how you used to laugh at the religious boys who looked at you with pity and disapproval for not covering up? And the others, the non-observant ones who followed us to the diner we always went to after the club. How they'd lecture you about eating pork, their breath still reeking from the alcohol they'd consumed without reservation. The way you bit on your greasy breakfast sausage, holding their gaze with a smirk that made them hate you and want you at the same time. I couldn't bridge the gap between that brilliant, gutsy, and outrageous girl I knew and what I feared you were becoming: austere, closed minded. Small.

For a while I hoped your newfound passion would be short-lived and that we'd eventually resume where we'd left off. Then, when I didn't hear from you, I started reading about Islam and the hijab. Why girls like you would seek refuge in religion, the intellectual pursuit it promises, the cultural bond it creates, the sense of meaning and purpose it provides. But I thought you and I already had these things and more. Only after your attack did I realize that my focus was misplaced. I couldn't see past my distaste for all things religious to register my own intolerance. I was too wrapped up in my fear of losing you to try to listen to your motivations or acknowledge that your piety doesn't negate my disbelief. I never wanted any deity — or any human being for that matter — to come between us. I wanted you and I to be like binary stars, forever linked by the gravitational force of our love for each other.

As Mark, Elaine, and I drove to your parents' place, I braced myself for rejection. *I might not be the friend she wants to see right now*, I told myself, *but I am the one she needs.* I rehearsed my apology: "I was selfish. I said mean things. I promise to do better." But most importantly, I wanted to tell you: "We're all that we got." And I hoped to hear you complete our mantra: "And that's not a small thing."

a kept woman

YASMIN STRAIGHTENS THE QUEEN-SIZE BED AS she makes arrangements to leave Ali, her husband of six years. With the phone tucked between her ear and shoulder, she brushes her palms over the duvet cover on her side of the bed, ridding it of the memory of her body.

"Hey, I'm on my way," Laura says from the other end of the line. "I had to pick up Nicky. She's snoring in the back."

Yasmin imagines Nicky, Laura's twenty-three-year-old roommate, recovering from yet another night of partying, her body curled on the tattered back seat of Laura's old Hyundai, her wavy red hair cascading down her face and onto the car floor like wine. Yasmin had been married to Ali for four years by the time she was

Nicky's age. She suddenly can't remember where her life has gone. She turns to face the bay window. Then her eyes drift to the tall, heavy bookshelf at the foot of her bed.

Sometimes at night, in that hazy state between wakefulness and dream, she believes an earthquake has hit the city — this is San Francisco after all — and she pictures the bookshelf crashing on top of her and pulverizing her bones and those of the baby she imagines she's carrying inside. She wakes up struggling to breathe through a constraining weight on her chest and sharp pains spreading from under her right breast toward her collarbone. The first time this happened, over a year ago, she turned to wake Ali, but she felt she was trying to reach out to a stranger, so she held back. Now that the midday sun has softened the bookshelf's edges a little, she feels bold enough to stare at it, in provocation almost, as if her nocturnal visions have infused the furniture with Ali's stocky, unyielding attributes.

"*A'udhu billahi!* Get a grip, you're yielding to *Shaidan*," her mother would have said, if she were there, clearing the air of evil spirits with Quranic words and sweeps of her *unsi*-perfumed shawl

Yasmin picks up her Canadian passport from Ali's chair. His desktop computer screen and open laptop sit side by side, facing her like a black-and-white portrait of a stern couple that brings to mind her parents' old wedding picture — the only one they'd managed to pack before they fled Somalia's civil war and settled in Ottawa when she was ten. She grabs a backpack and a small suitcase stuffed with her clothes and takes a deep breath, gathering strength from the memory of what happened just a few hours ago.

"Get out of my sight or *wallahi*, I'm going to flatten your face," Ali had said, swinging his fist so close to her face that, for a second, when she noticed the absence of pain in her body, she'd believed she must have been unconscious.

She unlocks the front door then turns back to face a large wood-framed mirror in the hallway of her small apartment. She ties her curly jet-black hair into a bun and quickly applies ChapStick on her thin lips. She looks around the room again. She detested the old, heavy furniture at first, but when they moved to San Francisco four years ago, they didn't want to buy nice things in case Ali's new job didn't pan out. After a while, Yasmin found the clutter comforting. It made her feel less alone when Ali worked late or went on business trips. These days, she loathes everything: the furniture, the gurgling of the baseboard heaters, the old building's musty air, the smell heightened and unrelenting in her mind, as though it carried tangible proof of her own inexorable decay.

She had been a first-year student at Algonquin College in Ottawa, pursuing a travel and tourism diploma when she first met Ali. She didn't know what she wanted to do once she graduated but she relished the idea of any job that would take her away from her parents. Two years earlier, her older sister, Hodan, had gotten pregnant at seventeen and run away to Vancouver with her boyfriend. Since then, their parents had been fatalistically waiting for another blow to crush their bruised expectations. "All of that for nothing," they'd been saying, conjuring up the memory of all the years they'd struggled in Canada as a refugee couple with no money, little education, and raising six young children. So Yasmin, the second-oldest child, was left to uphold her family's honour and hopes for a better future.

The night she met Ali, she was at a restaurant with a friend. Ali was there: older, well-spoken, and distinguished looking in his dark suit-and-tie ensemble. In contrast to guys her age, he had steady, knowing eyes.

"In this country, you have to blend in and work hard or you'll be left behind, doomed to slowly rot like roadkill," he'd told her with a slightly less-pronounced accent than her parents'.

Later on that night, as she took out her hijab from her backpack and covered her head and neck with it— right before her bus turned into Alta Vista Drive, five blocks away from her parents' house—she'd decided to marry him. He was Somali and educated, so she knew her parents would approve. Plus, he was liberal, she had deduced from their brief conversation, not the kind of Muslim man who'd impose head covering or other religious shenanigans on his wife. He was going to be her ticket out of her parents' stifling grip and a life steeped in a miasmic fog of superstition and sorrow.

On weekends, they drove downtown for lunch at the ByWard Market or stopped by one of the food trucks on Metcalfe Street for beef or chicken burgers before they went to the Rideau Centre to window shop or see a movie.

"It's not about religion," Ali had said to her when she once tried to get spicy Italian sausage instead of a beef burger. "Pigs are filthy animals. They eat their own shit." And Yasmin became someone who disapproved of pork for sanitary reasons.

Another time he said: "Alcohol is unnatural. Think about it. Have you ever seen an animal willingly drink alcohol?" Yasmin had never been around any animal to have noticed this, but it made sense, so she stopped drinking.

Once they got married, he often took her to functions and couples' outings with his colleagues from Nortel where he worked as a software engineer. She saw pride on his face then. Her Canadian accent spoke of his integration, her youth and beauty of his status. Once in a while, on these outings, Ali would share a bottle of wine, a pitcher of beer, or a pepperoni pizza with his colleagues without hesitation.

"When in Rome," he'd whispered to her the first time this happened. With his accent, the expression sounded off.

"You don't have to drink," he'd explained later. "Nobody would find a woman suspicious for not drinking, but I have to play the part. I can't afford to stand out, at least not yet. These people wouldn't understand."

She didn't attribute this justification to a weakness of character as her sister would have. In Yasmin's eyes, this was another quality that set Ali apart from her parents. It was proof of his ability to think things through logically and strategically, and to compromise when necessary, which made her feel closer to him. She loved it when he took her to Dow's Lake, where they'd sit in the sun and feed the ducks from their picnic basket. She would put her head on his shoulder and sigh, validated. It wasn't what she'd been longing for since before she could ever remember. It wasn't the passion of *Love and Basketball* or *Love Jones* she'd dreamed about in her early teens. But she found romance and certainty in these moments and in the way Ali let her hold his hand when they walked or the way he lightly kissed her forehead when he came home after she'd gone to bed.

This was before she quit school and followed him to San Francisco and before he started coming home later and later, his body looking ever more broken, as if he'd spent his days toiling in a cornfield instead of in

an ergonomic chair at a highly lauded software engin-
eering company.

"You should see those kids, Yasmin," he'd said then,
speaking of his new colleagues, his forehead wrinkling
like ripples at low tide. "You'd think they were brought
up on some wild animal's milk. I have to keep up or
else..."

This was before they stopped talking, before he
started looking at her with glazed eyes that made her
think the sight of her aggravated his tiredness.

"HEY JAZ, I need to use your bathroom," Laura says,
bursting into the apartment. Without waiting for a
reply, she engulfs Yasmin's narrow frame in her strong
arms. "Are you okay?"

Yasmin nods and points to the bathroom.

Laura runs, almost pushing Yasmin out of her way.

Yasmin's eyes follow the back of Laura's closely
cropped, dyed-blond hair, stiff and yellow like dry
grass against her dark brown skin. She gazes at her
own reflection in the mirror. She tucks a few loose curls
behind her ears and takes a deep breath again. Her lips
curve into a tentative smile as her anxiety subsides a
little, like the easing of a suffocating tropical heat. For
reasons she can't fully explain, Laura's presence always
has a soothing effect on her—something about the way
Laura looks at her with conviction, the way Laura's

firm hugs make her feel solid, whole. Yasmin has not experienced this kind of easy and invigorating relationship with another woman since Hodan left home nine years ago. She wonders what her sister would think of Laura. The two certainly exude a sense of urgency toward life that seems to escape her.

Yasmin met Laura at the San Francisco Carnaval about six months ago. Leaning against a residential building in the shade, Yasmin was watching throngs of people coming and going past food booths with clever names such as Curry Up Now and Hongry Kong. Smoke from barbecue grills and Indian clay ovens danced in the sun to the rhythms of salsa, tango, and reggae music blasting from giant speakers. Everything and everybody seemed to be rubbing and colliding against each other without any need for or interest in her.

"Hey, whatcha doin' there with all that space around you all to yourself?" Laura had shouted from a stand a few feet away. "Come and join the commotion," she'd said, waving her tattooed arms, her dark skin shining in the heat.

Yasmin couldn't remember the last time a stranger in San Francisco had talked to her with such familiarity and warmth. She went to Laura without any reservation, as though she was obeying a higher power. She helped Laura collect donations and sell T-shirts for a women's shelter. And she watched her haggle and banter with customers and passersby, captivated by her loud, jovial voice and the freedom that seemed embedded in her wide, energetic movements, as though Laura had never known the weight of modesty or the confinements of womanhood. That night, back in her apartment, Yasmin looked at her own body in the mirror, stretching her arms over her head and to her sides, awkwardly pirouetting, trying to imagine what it must feel like to yield to your own body, to take up space as naturally as Laura did. A few weeks later she started volunteering at the women's shelter with Laura.

"Alright, you have everything you need?" Laura asks as she comes out of the washroom, clapping her hands. "Ready to go?"

"Ready," Yasmin says, trying to match Laura's enthusiasm.

"You're doing the right thing," Laura says as she opens the front door.

"Actually, just a sec," Yasmin says and runs back into the bedroom.

She pulls off the duvet and sheets, throws them in a heap in the middle of the bed with the pillows, and looks at the result with satisfaction before walking out of the bedroom.

"Thanks again for letting me stay at your place," Yasmin says as the building's heavy door closes behind them.

Here and there, splotches of a mustardy-yellow

paint betray the two-storey building's former glory; now most of it has turned a dusty brown colour. The middle-aged Mexican woman in the next building yells something in Spanish from her window. Her son, a ten-year-old with clothes big enough to fit three of him at once, runs down Cesar Chavez Street with only a wave of the back of his hand. Yasmin stares at the woman for a moment while slowly rubbing her flat belly to soothe an ache she's just found there.

As they take their seats in the car, Laura points with her chin at Nicky's inert body in the back seat and says, "Apparently she drank too much last night, if that's even possible."

Yasmin usually enjoys Nicky's devil-may-care attitude, but today her presence irks her. "Sooo, yo, Jaz, I heard you finally left your ol' man," she imagines Nicky saying in a hushed tone when she wakes up, turning the whole thing into a high school gossip session. Or, "Sooo, are you ready for fresh meat?" she'll ask with a shrill laugh that always makes Yasmin think of a knife scratching on glassware.

Laura starts the engine and, singing along to Skunk Anansie's "Because of You," zigzags through the Mission Street traffic toward the west side of the city as though she were on her way to save someone's life.

YASMIN AND ALI had established early on they'd wait
a few years before having children, at least until she
finished school. Once in San Francisco, she wanted to
wait until Ali secured a work visa that would allow her
to seek employment or until they received the green
cards they'd applied for so she could resume school first.
At the beginning, since she didn't have a routine of her
own yet, setting herself up to Ali's schedule had made
her feel that she had an active role in building their new
life together. She woke up with him and cooked breakfast and dinner for two even though his job provided
free meals all day, hoping he would eventually miss
home-cooked foods. She ironed his clothes, cleaned the
apartment. On weekends, she made *anjero* with ghee
and honey, and tea with cinnamon, cloves, cardamom,
and whole milk the way her mother did for her father,
but Ali preferred fried eggs and coffee.

"Somali food is too rich, not healthy," he'd say, shaking his head as if he were the first of his countrymen to
have discovered this universal truth.

Although Yasmin thought the notion of completely
excising traditional foods from one's diet to achieve a
modern lifestyle ridiculous, something about the pride
of husbands she'd learned from her mother prevented
her from arguing against him.

Eventually, she gave in to pressure.

"Do you want to be like those white women with ten
degrees and no children?" her father said half-jokingly

at first, his voice raspy from decades of smoking.

"Who's going to take care of you in your old age, *Hooyo*?" her mother pleaded.

Ali agreed. "I make enough money for both of us now," he said. "Besides, it's not just about you." There was an accusation in his eyes and a demand for reparation in his tone—reparation for something she'd done as much for his sake as for her own; for something he'd continued to refuse to even acknowledge had happened let alone discuss since before they'd moved to San Francisco.

"HEY, CHEER UP. He was bound to find out eventually and now it's done," Laura says, shifting gears as they near a red light.

"I don't know how I'm going to tell my parents about it."

"You know, sometimes, you just have to blurt it out and let them deal with it."

"What I did is unforgivable. They wanted grandchildren so badly. They'll side with him."

"He almost hit you."

"But he didn't."

"So? Anyway, parents are all the same. Sooner or later, they'll come around. My parents didn't talk to me for years after I came out to them."

"It's not the same." Yasmin interrupts Laura with

a sharper tone than she intended. When she turns to apologize, she catches a devastating expression in Laura's eyes. She remembers what Laura had told her about her own parents—how they'd tried to beat what they called "the Devil" out of her for months until she ran away from home at sixteen. For the first time, Yasmin realizes that, despite her alluring sense of freedom and her confident exterior, Laura could be as vulnerable as anyone else. "I'm sorry, Laura, I didn't mean to be rude. I know you're trying to help but..."

"No worries," Laura says.

Yasmin wishes she knew words fluid enough to convey to Laura what seeing the old spectre of failure and disgrace—that silent companion of all displaced people—on her parents' faces will do to her. And what the yoke of faintly veiled scorn and pity from others will do to her family as the news reaches the whole community with the speed of a calamity.

They stay quiet for a while, the space between them expanding with the distance of otherness. The music turns to silence as well, as if in reverence.

"Anyway, divorce is now inevitable, which means I'll lose my visa, so I'll have to go back and live with them until I find a job. I don't have the luxury of time and distance to wait until they come around."

"You can stay at my place as long as you need to, okay?" Laura says, reaching out and squeezing Yasmin's shoulder.

Yasmin sinks back in her seat and leans against the car's door frame. She follows absentmindedly the rows of rundown Victorian houses, the old road in dire need of repair, shop-owners piling up colourful fruits and vegetables on stands in front of their stores, small-time street vendors and hustlers selling trinkets to tourists and locals. Her mind lingers at the sight of yet another handful of Latino migrant workers standing at a street corner. In a way, she is one of them. Her stay in the United States depends on someone else's whim and she's far from a home she dreads going back to.

THE FIRST TIME she thought of leaving Ali was a year after they'd started trying for a baby. Ali had come home early that day and was at the dining table eating the food he'd brought from work in a Styrofoam container. She'd watched his stooped body from the living room for a while: the tired motion with which he stabbed grilled chicken and vegetables with his fork, the way he chewed his food, his wide-set, small, droopy eyes and his receding hairline elongating his face. He made her think of an old goat. She felt pity.

"Ali, *Macaan*...I think this country is destroying us. Without work or school, I feel useless. I thought I could handle waiting but..." She stopped. She wasn't sure going back to Canada would solve their problems anymore. All she was certain of was that she hated her life: her status as Ali's dependent; the idle solitude; expecting to be pregnant every month and not knowing whether she should feel relieved or sad when she found out she wasn't.

He sighed and dropped his fork in the container. "It said right on the forms you signed: 'It takes five to six years for a green card,' remember?" he said, with the tone of someone addressing a capricious child.

"Let's go back. I know you're unhappy here too. This job is killing you."

"I'm fine," he said, his voice a decibel louder. His tone had a forcefulness to it that betrayed a desperate obstinacy.

"We could own a house for the rent we pay for this mouldy apartment," she added.

"Oh, now this apartment is not good enough for you?" His eyes were beads constrained in narrow slits.

"No, that's not..."

She sat there watching him chew his food again, hoping he'd say something more, something she could counter. She then focused her attention on a bruised spot on the doorway leading to the kitchen. The thick layers of beige paint that had coagulated on the frame over the years made it look like splattered, viscous batter. After a while, she went and stood in front of her husband.

"Come on, baby," she said.

He put down his fork again and leaned back in his

chair. He looked her up and down slowly and, dragging his words, said: "I don't know what you're complaining about. A lot of girls would be happy to be in your shoes. I'm the one stuck with a barren woman."

"There is nothing wrong with me. I was able to...," she said and stopped. The memory of her first pregnancy and the overwhelming bitterness hidden deep within it was robbing her of words.

He held her stare for a moment before he waved her away and went back to eating.

As she turned to leave, Ali's last words entered her consciousness, slowly, as though she could still believe she'd misinterpreted his meaning, the way one questions a traumatic childhood experience. She wondered if this was his way of getting back at her for something she wasn't aware of. Then, the words expanded and multiplied in her head with the force of a violent wave crashing before they were distilled into a single new awareness: she was an expendable, kept woman. His family could find him another wife in a heartbeat. She felt as if she were caught in a wild wind and had lost both her sense of direction and balance. She stood there in front of him for a while in an attempt to steady herself, then went to bed quietly, one hand pressing her chest where a piercing pain was starting to make itself known.

She swore she'd leave him then, but didn't. By morning, the thought of returning to her parents' house a divorcee had spread in her mind like a sudden bout of migraine.

"Did he beat you? Then, what's wrong?" She imagined her mother's wronged face behind the melodramatic voice at the other end of the line. And her dad pacing in their living room, tightening his *ma'awis* on his waist with quick, sharp gestures, occupying himself with the adjustment and readjustment of his wrapper to defuse his exasperation.

She pictured Hodan's I-told-you-so look. "How can you stand this FOB? He'll never shed his country ways. Why can't you just live for yourself for once?" she'd said when she came to visit eight months earlier.

"As you did?" Yasmin wanted to say but didn't. She had just recently admitted to herself how much she resented her sister for having deserted her, for having left her to deal with their parents' anger and shame, but she hadn't yet built up the conviction she needed to voice this.

At first, she only eavesdropped on Ali's conversations with his mother. Then she got into the habit of sifting through his emails and text message exchanges with his brothers whenever she could, until one morning, she caught her own reflection in the mirror, the dark circles around her eyes and her halo of tangled, unkempt hair. She saw the needy, frantic woman she'd become. She decided there and then to change but didn't know how to go about it.

For a while, she went to the public library on Bartlett and 24th Street. She marvelled at the archways and columns of the old building and walked the length of each aisle, the tips of her fingers brushing against the rows of books. Although she had never been much one to read, she thought she could learn to enjoy it but, with all those books at her disposal, she didn't know where to start.

"What about Nuruddin Farah?" suggested an old friend from Ottawa she still talked to from time to time. Yasmin was annoyed at herself for not having thought of it on her own. After all, Nuruddin Farah was the most popular Somali writer alive. Wanting to do things properly, she set out to read Farah's books in chronological order, starting with *From a Crooked Rib*. But after she'd struggled through half the book, all that stayed with her was the loneliness of childbirth and the blood and stink of the aftermath: the heat, flies, and rotting umbilical cord. These images only made her own struggles with pregnancy more painful.

Ali was changing too. He started attending Friday prayers in the city, reading the Quran on weekends, taking trips to Ottawa for family visits without her. Yasmin observed these changes but only peripherally, the way one catches glimpses of images on a TV screen while waiting in line at the bank. For by then, she'd found an outlet for her solitude and ennui: Facebook. She became hooked on the semblance of friendship and connection it offered, until the never-ending exhibition of success and excitement plastered all over the web site heightened her unhappiness.

That's when the walls started to cave in on her. When she and Ali were having sex, she was not sure if it was her he was pressing himself against anymore. She saw a part of herself hovering on the ceiling, watching; she saw bodies, movements; she heard panting; she smelled sweat. All of it was there and yet not there, like watching a dismembered doll where a human should be. She then started ensconcing herself in the bathroom where she'd spend hours pulling out hair from her head, yanking one or a few strands at a time, focusing all her empty thoughts on that moment before the sting, savouring the prickle to come until she lost her footing completely and drifted away in her mind, slowly, imperceptibly, her idle days bleeding into each other, then into weeks and months.

NICKY SITS CROSS-LEGGED on the living room floor of the apartment she shares with Laura and places burritos, tortilla chips, and salsa on the coffee table in front of Yasmin.

"Eat," she says, reaching into the paper bag for a tortilla chip.

"Thanks, Nicky. You didn't have to. How much do I owe you?" Yasmin says and takes a bite of her breakfast burrito. The chunks of fried egg, beans, and avocado protruding from the wrap melt in her mouth, easing her stomach's growling.

"It's on me. You've been cooking for us the last three weeks. And I got good tips last night," Nicky says with a mischievous smile.

Two weeks ago, Yasmin watched Nicky with fascination as she poured drinks and flirted with her customers, her every move and gesture — even the act of wiping the bar counter clean — charged with overt, inviting sexuality. Yasmin had never thought working as a bartender could be an empowering job for a woman, yet she could not deny the element of control and even fun the interplay between Nicky and her customers elicited.

That's the bar where Yasmin had met Jason. He'd reminded her of the boys she used to know at Algonquin College, before she met Ali. As Jason conveyed his interest in her over the cacophony of the Friday night crowd, a mix of beer and mint on his breath, she remembered with sadness how she used to look down on guys like him, how she used to equate their forced bravado and flimsy attempt at seduction with an irreparable intellectual and moral flaw. So when she agreed to meet up with him at Dolores Park a few days later, she thought of it not as a date, but as a chance at redemption for her old snobbery.

She was watching couples cuddling on beach towels when he came to sit beside her. To her surprise, she felt gleeful. Unbeknown to herself, she had missed him. The view of downtown San Francisco in the distance took on a different hue. It pleased her to think that, in the eyes of passersby, she and Jason could be seen as a couple. The fog building up in the hills behind her carried a mysterious, romantic note.

"How is volunteering working out for ya?" Nicky's voice interrupts her thoughts.

"It puts things in perspective," Yasmin says, her eyes on a pile of zines on the carpet under the coffee table. *Sex Workers, Health and Safety*, she reads.

Sometimes, Yasmin watches the women at the shelter while she empties cans of Chef Boyardee ravioli into a big pan to heat up for lunch or pours ketchup on a bland meatloaf before she serves it for dinner. There is Diane, a sturdy woman of forty who spends her time between meals at the same corner table, shuffling a deck of cards, mumbling and gesturing at an invisible opponent; Alex, chatty and barely out of teenagehood and yet her body already criss-crossed with scars of drug abuse and street life; and Edwidge, who smokes cigarettes through her nostrils for the pain it causes her. Their tales are of unspeakable, heart-wrenching damages but also of survival and resilience.

"I bet. Did I ever tell you Laura saved my life?" Nicky says before she engulfs a chip in her crimson-painted mouth.

Yasmin shakes her head.

"We've known each other since high school. You knew that, right?"

Yasmin nods.

"Anyway, I had this asshole for a boyfriend. He was abusive but I was totally under his spell. I couldn't leave him. Laura was having a lot of problem with her folks too. Her dad was ... Well, she couldn't be herself in a hick town in Montana. You know that part. One day, she just came up to me after school and said, 'Do you wanna move to San Francisco together?' And that was that. If it wasn't for her, I'd probably have ended up in a ditch somewhere."

Yasmin can't imagine Nicky under anyone's spell except her own. Is it possible she'd read Nicky wrong? Do we ever really know people?

She once thought she knew Ali too. Two months before they were to move to San Francisco, she'd gotten pregnant. They were in bed when she told Ali. He stayed silent for a while. She wished she'd told him while the lights were still on so she could read his face.

"It's bad timing, right?" she said to break the silence.

"That's what I was thinking too." He cleared his throat. "This job, it's a once-in-a-lifetime opportunity. And it's going to be hard, you know. Moving to a new country ..."

"I know," she said.

"I don't know if we'll have health insurance coverage right away. If, God forbid, you have a difficult pregnancy. Anyway, let's talk about it tomorrow, okay?" he said and turned to sleep.

She rested her thoughts on the cadence of his light snore to avoid confounding her confusion with speculations.

The next day, she waited for him to say something. Then waited for two more weeks, replaying his last words on the subject in her mind again and again, as though he had spoken in riddles, before she gave up and booked an appointment at the clinic.

It wasn't the act itself she found hard to bear later. She'd done what she'd had to do for the good of her marriage. The snare of tradition, religion, and the validation that offspring bring to a marriage — she'd believed she and Ali were above these things. Wasn't that why she'd married him? They would start a family when they were both ready, she'd told herself. But she had expected him to show sympathy and gratitude toward her for having been brave enough to have gone through the abortion on her own. A loving, comforting word would have sufficed. Instead, Ali looked the other way. He cut her off with random work-related anecdotes whenever she broached the subject. That's when it first occurred to her that her husband might not be the enlightened man she'd believed him to be.

"Sometimes, you're too practical, too *cadaan*," her mother used to say, complaining about Yasmin's Western ways.

Although Yasmin wasn't going to put this into words for another four years yet, deep in her heart, that was the time when Ali stopped being her life partner and became instead a placeholder for a life she had yet to imagine.

Nicky cleans her fingers with a paper napkin, smearing the Chipotle logo with a red and green mixture of condiments, then takes out a pack of cigarettes and a lighter from her jacket pocket.

"Can I have one?" Yasmin asks.

"I didn't know you smoked," Nicky says, passing her the pack.

"I did. When I was a teenager. Before I got married." Yasmin takes her first puff and exhales, satisfied. "Oh God, I'm so dizzy," she says, rubbing her eyes with her hands and shaking her head.

"Oh, how I miss that first-time high," Nicky says.

They laugh and continue smoking in silence. Yasmin leans her head against the couch, relishing their nascent friendship.

JASON MAKES YASMIN feel that she's the centre of his world. He waits for her at the end of her shift at the shelter, calls her a few times a day just to say he misses her. She admires his intrepid activism. The way he shares his outrage at the state of humanity makes her feel that she too can be part of something important;

that she is capable not only of taking control of her own life but also of transcending her limitations to become part of the world around her. In a way, he reminds her of Laura: he's knowledgeable, supportive, and not domineering.

Yasmin found it so easy to talk to Jason that she didn't hold anything back. When she told him about her imminent divorce, she discerned a hint of titillation, a secret smile only made visible by the slight lift of the slanted outer edges of his eyes. She told him she left her husband the day he found the birth control pills she'd been secretly taking as one would take medication for a serious heart condition. She started taking the pills when he insinuated, a year earlier, that he could easily find himself another wife.

"You fucking murderer! You killed my baby and all this time, all this time you've been depriving me of another chance to have a child. You degenerate, spoiled bitch!" Ali had yelled, waving the pill dispenser in front of her. The contents of the makeup case where she'd been hiding the pills were spilled on the bathroom floor. "Disgracing yourself with that drunken whore. And that . . . that . . ." He'd broken off — as if it would have been too disgusting and beneath him to voice what he thought of Laura — before he emptied the contraceptive pill dispenser in the toilet.

Yasmin told Jason how Ali's bellowing, the venom in his voice, had reminded her of the day she came home late once when she was a teenager and found her dad on the couch, in their living room, his bandaged leg resting high on a pillow. He had slipped and sprained his ankle at the Quickie where he worked when he ran on the wet floor he'd just mopped to catch teenagers who'd shoplifted from the store. Her father had screamed at her: "Where have you been? Whoring?" He'd writhed about and cursed in such a way that made Yasmin wonder if he were struck by a sudden mortal blight.

"Immigrant men of a certain age face a particular kind of problem," Jason told her with the serious face of a concerned academic. He had taken her hand in his while she related her story. "Many are brought up to be the sole breadwinners and decision-makers for their families. When they come here, oftentimes, they are stripped of their status, social and professional. So these kinds of incidents add to that sense of humiliation and loss of control. And men rarely reach out for help, so we hear a lot of cases of depression, alcoholism, and violent behaviour."

Yasmin didn't appreciate having her life presented to her as a social study case. She wanted to negate Jason's assertions, show disdain for his I'm-in-the-business-of-saving-immigrants-from-themselves attitude. She wanted to tell him her father and Ali were not mere statistical data he could compile and manipulate to impress her. Instead, she withdrew her hand and vowed not to see him again.

But when she met Ali a month later to discuss the
details of the divorce, she couldn't help but think about
Jason's words. Her eyes stopped on the dark spot on
her husband's forehead: the mark of daily prayers he'd
fervently taken up in the last year. Ali had traded his
weekend baseball hats for a Muslim skullcap and his
weekly tennis matches for visits to the local mosque:
"To atone for your sin and mine," he'd told her with a
resigned voice. Facing the fact of the abortion had pre-
cipitated the collapse of the elusive American dream
he'd been chasing in the last twenty years he'd lived
in North America. She saw a disillusioned, ageing man
who, despite his education and financial success, was
grappling now with the same concerns as her parents:
trying to salvage something of the past, to find, in the
faith of his upbringing, something that would absolve
him of his sins and give his life a new meaning.

YASMIN FOLDS UP Laura's sofa-bed where she's been
sleeping for the past two months and follows Laura
and Nicky out of the apartment.

"So, excited to finally go to Outside Lands?" Nicky
says. "I can't believe you haven't been to one yet. That
husband of yours must've been keeping you in a dun-
geon or somethin'."

"Ha ha. Ali was just, you know, always busy."
Yasmin's voice trails off.

"Yeah, and you felt too guilty to go out without him. Blah blah. Anyway, I'm just teasing ya. You're really easy to get, you know that?" Nicky says, laughing.

With a detachment that surprises her, Yasmin imagines Ali with a devout wife. A decent, God-fearing woman. Someone who'd understand him better than she ever could. One not prone to depression and less inclined to moral dilly-dallying. A woman who'd make herself bend when necessary so that her husband might feel tall. Someone capable of embracing motherhood and tradition. A woman who'd gather in her house and in her heart a long line of extended family. Someone who'd be there for the ill and the bereaved in her community. A woman like her own mother.

"Today you're gonna see why SF is the birthplace of hippie," Laura says as they take their seats in her car.

"Sex, drugs, and rock 'n' roll, huh?" Yasmin asks.

"Nah," Laura says. "Love, my friend, love. And music, freedom, and, hopefully, some sun." The silver-coated clouds cover the sky like one big sheet of cotton wool.

"By the way, my boss has agreed to meet with you," Laura continues. "You're a good cook and a clean freak. I'm sure he'll hire you. I think some of the guys in the kitchen are illegals." Laura's hands leave the steering wheel for a second to put *illegals* in quotation marks. "Whatcha say, huh? I think you'd look pretty sexy in a kitchen uniform," she says, slapping Yasmin's back and laughing in a way that always uplifts Yasmin's mood.

"I'm liking the volunteering thing," Yasmin says. "It's cathartic. But working under the table sounds sketchy. Ali has agreed to let me keep my credit card until the divorce is finalized, so for now, I'm going to enjoy SF a little then return home."

"Naah, you're staying right here with us. We'll find a way," Laura says, leaning in and encircling Yasmin's frail shoulders with a strong grip.

For a second, Yasmin sees a certain kind of anguish in Laura's eyes—something like a melancholy borne out of a futile yearning. The intensity of the expression frightens Yasmin a little. She wonders if things would have been different if she were like Laura, but her imagination can't stretch far enough to fathom such a possibility. She always wanted to be financially independent, of course, but never envisaged she, or any other woman, for that matter, could lead a fulfilled, happy life without a man by her side. She didn't care much for the sanctity of marriage but she believed in the complementarity of man and woman the way she believed in the interdependence of night and day, sky and earth.

"That's binary bullshit," Laura had said once. Yasmin wasn't sure what that meant so she'd left it alone. But what she knows, what her friendship with Laura and Nicky has taught her is that there is more than one way of being a woman and of finding happiness.

"Besides, Ottawa is too cold and I bet it's boring," Laura says.

"I'm going to Vancouver," Yasmin says.

"Same difference."

After the initial outburst of criticism and tears, her parents had quickly geared themselves into damage control mode.

"Can you find a way to stay there?" they'd asked. Then, "Go to your sister's. I know someone. We'll figure something out."

Yasmin had imagined her mother mentally sifting through the list of divorcees and widowers she knew, but there was no point dissuading the old woman from trying to find another husband for her. Yasmin knew the worst was behind her, and that was good enough for now.

AFTER DRIVING AROUND Golden Gate Park for a while in search of a free parking space, Laura settles for a spot on Sunset Boulevard, ten blocks away from their destination. They have left the grit of the Mission District behind. Here, the lawns and hedges in front of the multi-coloured houses are trimmed and the wide median strips are lined with Monterey cypress trees.

"There has to be a way. Maybe Jason can marry you," Nicky says as they turn onto Lincoln Way. "What's going on with you two anyway?"

Music from behind Golden Gate Park's giant trees fuses with the enthusiasm of concertgoers swelling around them. Yasmin knows sleeping with Jason would mean sealing shut any possibility of going back to her old life with Ali, and that should be motivation enough, but she knows she can't get involved with someone to get out of a tight situation again. This only really dawned on her the day she left Ali. Before calling Laura for help — Ali had gone to work by then — she'd sat in her living room for an hour mulling over what had happened. She had, through depression and beyond, never forgotten to take her pills: it was the only concrete thing she had ever done for herself. For everything else, she'd always counted on someone else to save her. She remembers how, back in Mogadishu, before the civil war forced her family to flee, she and Hodan would practise new dance moves watching bootleg tapes of Paula Abdul and Janet Jackson until their parents came home or the scratched-up tape got caught in the vhs player. They'd then spend the rest of their day dreaming up ways to run away to America to become superstars like their idols. There was an unspoken understanding that Hodan would make that dream come true for both of them. Isn't that what older sisters were supposed to do? Their dreams were boundless back then.

"Jason is nice, but it's too early," Yasmin says. "The divorce is not even finalized. And I need to learn to take care of myself on my own."

"So?" Nicky says. "Stop pining away. He could be your perfect rebound fling. He's so hot. I'd totally do him."

"See? Girl, you need to stay right here where poetry and debauchery rule," Laura says and starts to run up ahead. She stops a block away, then turns back and runs toward her friends, her arms wide open, the wind blowing the sleeves of her white tracksuit jacket. She lifts Yasmin off the ground, carries her up the hill for a second then puts her back down.

"Come on, lazy bum, work those legs. You're twenty-five, not fifty," she says and runs ahead again.

Yasmin runs after Laura for a block then stops for a moment to catch her breath and unwrap the scarf her mother gave her. She looks up toward the gate's entrance and waves the scarf at Laura. The turquoise, pink, and yellow of the cloth swim in the air like the lavish life hidden under her parents' piece of the Red Sea. It's Ali's and her Red Sea too. She knows this will never change. But as she contemplates the possibility of a new life free of the constraints of her parents' — and Ali's — world, she can't help feeling anxious that she might forget this. That she might drift so far away from her roots that she'll lose sight of all that is also beautiful and true about her upbringing: the complicated but genuine love of family, the tenderness and laughter, the safety of community, the poetry embedded in her mother tongue. Could she salvage these things and still achieve the freedom and autonomy she's always wanted? And will she really fit in in this other world? Or will she be subjected to a different set of constraints?

She remembers something Laura had told her about W. E. B. Du Bois's book *The Souls of Black Folk* and the concept of double consciousness. And how this concept is sometimes applied to immigrants' experience of feeling permanently in exile, stuck on the threshold between the cultures of their origin and those of their new home. Yasmin stands there lost in thought, trying to remember more about this conversation, to find an answer to her dilemma in it, until she notices that Laura is still waving at her. It dawns on her then that even in exile, we sometimes stumble upon a path, a new way forward. And we find strength and friendship in the most unlikely of travel companions.

As she presents her ticket to the attendant at the gate, she sees Jason standing a few feet away. She turns to Nicky, who responds with a wink. Yasmin looks at Jason again. She takes in his secretive smile. The intense way he looks at her causes her heart to skip a beat. She feels a new kind of excitement grow in her, an unburdened, daring energy. She doesn't care about Jason's intentions or what it all means anymore. She will follow him home tonight.

She turns around and locks arms with Nicky.

"Thanks, these shoes are not made for hiking," Nicky says.

Yasmin looks at Nicky's five-inch pumps and smiles. For now, she's just glad her own shoes are comfortable enough she can lend a hand to a friend.

things are good now

THE FIRST TIME MY SISTER, ALEM, TALKED ABOUT her time in prison, it was 1981, about two weeks after she came to Toronto via Sudan, where she'd spent a year at a refugee camp. We were in my old apartment in North York.

"We were up to thirty women in a small cell," she said, staring out the curtainless window.

The lazy afternoon sun spread its blue-grey hue on her light-brown complexion, blurring the contours of her angular face. I wanted to hug her or hold her hands, but I stayed put. She had flinched when I'd tried earlier, something about having spent too much time in the proximity of death, so I just sat there rubbing the stubble on my chin and remembering the general euphoria following the 1974 coup against Emperor

Haile Selassie. And how, a few years later, millions of Ethiopians watched the new government, the Derg, swiftly dismantle the last of their dreams and hopes in breathless horror, as if they were collectively suffering from a collapsed lung.

"Every couple of days, they'd call someone's name. They'd take you to an interrogation room, beat you to a pulp with fists, leather straps, anything. Or use you as a human ashtray," she continued in a low voice.

I had heard about interrogation centres and firing squads at police stations around Addis Ababa, gunshots echoing in the night, prisoners scrubbing blood off dirty walls in the cold violet light of dawn; parents scrambling to pay for the bullets used to "weed out the enemies of the Revolution," as the new regime called the executions, so they could retrieve their children's remains for a proper burial lest the dead be thrown into an anonymous mass grave or left to rot in the streets.

I also knew about the hundreds of samizdat the underground resistance distributed at night, the kind that cost Alem two years of her life.

Our mother had sent me a letter with Alem. "I know my daughter, she's holding back," she wrote. "Please talk to her. She needs to let all that poison out." Mother was right. I had heard Alem struggle with nightmares. She moaned and cried in her sleep. I had even heard her mumble her own name once or twice, but I didn't let it penetrate my mind beyond superficially noting its strangeness. I had caught her many times staring at things, too, her body petrified mid-action in some mundane chore, her mind lost in a realm beyond my reach. I didn't ask questions, too afraid of what I might learn. How could I, her brother, have asked what young cadres brimming with the insolence of a newly acquired ideology and power could have done to a seventeen-year-old girl in their custody? How could I have asked, when Alem's bourgeois upbringing alone was loathsome enough to the Derg to justify any punishment, even death? So instead of forming questions, I tried to close the rift that her imprisonment had cleaved between us.

"You are safe now," I said. "You have your whole life ahead of you."

Alem turned to me with a perplexed look. She was twenty but her deep-set eyes had the gravitas of someone twice her age.

"They're slaughtering children, for God's sake, Benny," she cried out. "The streets are littered with corpses."

Only my immediate family and childhood friends back home called me Benny. To everyone else, I was Beniam or Ben. The sound of my nickname solidified her presence in the room.

"You were only fifteen when I left, and nobody thought they'd go after women and children. Otherwise, I would have taken you with me," I said. Thoughts of my own escape five years earlier flooded my mind: the walk across the border into Kenya, the interminable stretch of land, the blisters, and the fear of capture a dark and tenacious shadow companion.

She covered her face with her hands for a moment. "I know, Benny," she said after a while, her crooked front teeth slightly visible under her thin lips, her voice gentle again, like a healing whiff of eucalyptus leaves.

I looked past her at the high-rise buildings across the street. My eyes followed earth-toned leaves to their final resting place at the foot of the majestic tree outside. "It's called a maple tree," my neighbour had told me when I came to Canada four years earlier in 1977. Toronto had felt like a strange new planet then: white faces everywhere I turned, rows of immaculate lawns leading up to identical brick houses. When I first saw the just-completed CN Tower, I couldn't believe it was humanly possible to build such a monument. It was as though I'd found a ladder into the heavens. It made me feel that anything was possible in Canada.

"Drink your tea before it gets cold," I said, taking a sip of mine. Cloves and cinnamon filled my nostrils, transporting me back to our childhood home, to the sky-blue walls of the small bedroom Alem and I shared when we were little, the cracks on its ceiling like an aerial view of the Nile. I wanted to tell her how, in the deep of the long and dark Canadian winter when the suspicious looks of landlords or the disdain in strangers' eyes clogged my soul, I longed for the warmth of our home. And how even the memory of my strife with Father, the man who'd called me a coward for leaving the country to escape imprisonment, couldn't dampen this longing. I wanted to reminisce about old times but I refrained—she didn't care for nostalgia.

ALEM FOUND SOME things difficult at first, of course, but she took to her new life faster than I'd expected. She appreciated the calm and reserved demeanour of Canadians, which she thought made them seem incapable of suspicion or belligerence. She worked long hours scrubbing pots and pans in one restaurant kitchen or another with the dedication of someone who'd always known they were destined to do just that. In the spring, she lined our little balcony with potted herbs and flowers. For a while, whenever we went to the grocery store, she insisted we go through each aisle, running her hands over the neatly packaged goods, her eyes leaping from one overflowing shelf to another as if only in that space could she believe she no longer had to wait in line at the *kebele,* government-issued ration card in hand for meagre allowances of basic necessities. But once in a while, this excitement would give way to a shroud of gloom.

"It's just not fair, is it?" she would say. "All this luxury. All this peace."

When I lived alone, I had only a mattress, sheets, and a few dishes. A week before Alem arrived, I'd furnished the apartment with a couch, a dining table and four chairs, a bed for her, a cassette player, and more dishes. Everything was second-hand, but I thought the furniture gave the apartment an air of respectability. With the spices she'd bought in Khartoum and improvising with what she could find in Indian stores in Toronto, Alem cooked us dishes that approximated food from home. With her beside me, I became a person again. In her I saw myself reflected, my name and roots restored. I was no longer a ghost.

I wanted to do all the things normal families did: go on trips, talk about our hopes and frustrations, invite friends to our home for dinner parties. But Alem was frugal with money and didn't care for friends or talk. She especially avoided fellow Ethiopians, choosing, if any, the company of immigrants from other countries.

"It's better this way. We don't need anyone meddling in our affairs," she explained once.

I wanted to point out that we didn't have much in the way of "affairs" that necessitated isolation but I let it slide. Whenever any of my *Habesha* friends dropped by the apartment, she turned stiff, resisting any attempt at familiarity, like a feral animal.

"Your sister is so reserved," they said, but I knew they meant she was a snob.

All in all, under the circumstances, I thought she

was adjusting fairly well, so I assumed it was just a matter of time. Even the nightmares seemed to have subsided, although she still slept with her bedroom door ajar and the light on.

ONE DAY, after Alem and I had been living together for six years, I invited Nick, Alem's boss, to dinner to thank him for giving her rides home whenever she worked late.

"This might be too spicy for a white man's palate," she said in the morning while stirring the *doro wet*. This was her way of telling me she disapproved of the invitation. The smell of *berbere* and spiced butter in the thick red-brown sauce had invaded all corners of the two-bedroom apartment we'd just moved into and carried out to the hall. I worried our neighbours would complain.

"Have you been back to Ethiopia yet?" Nick asked, sitting on the edge of his chair, kneading its corduroy-covered seat with his fist as if to scratch an itch.

I poured him a glass of Johnnie Walker.

"Not yet. Plane tickets are expensive," I said, taking a sip of my whisky.

Nick watched my sister's brisk walk to and from the kitchen, his eyes lingering. I imagined him following her around Swiss Chalet's kitchen, teaching her how to turn powder starch she had mistaken for flour into mashed potatoes or inspecting the storage rooms she had just cleaned while making jokes she didn't quite understand or care about.

Alem poured various meat and vegetable dishes onto the *injera* on our plates.

"Alem told me you study modern art," he said.

"Yes. I also work at Loblaws."

"Good, good . . . I study political science at the University of Toronto," he volunteered with obvious pride. "Only part-time though."

I nodded, my mouth too full to speak.

"You know, Alem is my best employee. She's never late, never sick. If I could only get more words than *hello* and *goodnight* out of her," he continued with a guttural laugh. "She'll make a fine nurse when she graduates." Beads of sweat were building around his widow's peak.

"This sauce is spicy, right? Have some more cheese. It will kill the sting," Alem said with a sudden wide smile.

A splash of crimson spread over Nick's tawny face.

"And what do you do for fun?" Nick asked me. "I know Alem doesn't believe in fun," he teased.

"I go for walks by the water sometimes. It's relaxing," she said, a slight defiance in her voice.

"Oh, Joseph told me he goes for strolls in the city too. You two should go for a walk by the lake sometime," Nick said, taking a quick gulp of whisky, his eyes on her.

A sturdy man of few words, Joseph was Alem's new co-worker from Haiti. He had escaped Duvalier's brutal regime with a scar that ran down his neck like an earth-worm crawling under his deep brown skin. Alem didn't talk much about him but I had sensed a bond transcend-ing words between them—broken people have ways of finding one another.

"Sure," she said, without looking up.

"I sometimes hang out with friends at an Ethiopian restaurant-bar on Bloor Street. It's called YeSheba Bet. Do you know it?" I asked.

Alem shook her head. "It's a place for people without a purpose in life. Sitting around all night, drinking and arguing about politics. A waste of time and money," she said, with a barely contained grumble in her voice.

Alem's life had been entrenched in chores and responsibilities for so long now that I often had dif-ficulty remembering the jaunty, coddled teenager she once was.

"Speaking of politics, I heard about your president on the BBC," Nick said. "They said he dismantled the old feudal system almost overnight, implemented land reforms..."

"Yes."

"And he sends college students to teach the illiterate masses in remote villages. That's good for the coun-try, right?" Nick said, his eyes eagerly waiting for an affirmation.

I looked at Alem out of the corner of my eye. She stared at Nick with pursed lips. She had lashed out at one of my friends before for complaining about the underground resistance's inefficiency, but that was a while back and the guy was a pompous ass anyway so I was proud of her when she put him in his place. She sometimes snapped at me for little things, too, but we'd managed to avoid serious altercations and I usually made sure to quickly quell any talk of politics around her. But I guess the alcohol was getting to me.

I said: "You see, the revolution was a good thing. People were tired of Emperor Haile Selassie's extravagances, and their demand for change had gone unheard for too long. But then, soon after taking control of the government, the Derg started killing or imprisoning all who questioned its authority, so —"

Nick interrupted me. "Yeah, they talked about that too. But you know, the way I see it, history is written by ambitious leaders who sometimes have to cheat and kill."

"Well, it doesn't —"

"Sometimes these countries need a strong man to clean shit up, don't you think?" Nick interrupted me again.

"He is an animal! Him and all his minions!" Alem shrieked in Amharic, scowling at Nick. The light from the cheap lamp hanging over the dining table exaggerated her glaring eyes. "Hundreds of thousands of people have been tortured and killed. Thousands disappeared without a trace," she continued, tapping the table with her index finger. "And you. What do you know? You wouldn't have lasted a day in those jails. You would have shat your pants," she said, now pointing her finger at him.

I translated her words, omitting the reference to prison, and got up to clear the table.

As if coming out of hypnosis, Alem put a plate she'd picked up back on the table, her hands trembling. She quickly mumbled an apology and disappeared into her bedroom.

"How about that, eh? I never thought I'd see Alem raise her voice," Nick said, his flushed face stretched into a wild grin hovering between fright and excitement.

After Nick left, I tried to focus my attention on a new class project. I opened my sketchbook and started to absentmindedly scribble in the corner of a page. Alem came out of her bedroom then stopped in her tracks with a look of surprise that made me wonder if she wished I had left with Nick. After a second or two that felt like an hour, she returned to her bedroom, slamming the door behind her.

I sat there staring at my sketchbook, downing one glass of whisky after another until I emptied the half-full bottle.

THREE YEARS LATER this girl I was dating, Julie, and I were on my balcony, smoking weed. I heard Julie say:

"Hey, Alem, care to join us?" My girlfriend had stretched her arm past my face to hand the burning joint to Alem with the silly smile of someone who was still recovering from deep laughter. I turned around to face my sister. It took me a moment to grasp the situation. Alem stood against the balcony door, one hand folded into a fist on her hip and staring at me in that way *Habesha* mothers have of terrorizing children into confession without uttering a word. I instinctively smacked Julie's hand away with the back of mine. The joint flew out of my girlfriend's fingers and over the balcony railing.

"Alem, sorry. I didn't think you...," I said, almost stammering before I stopped. I realized I was too high and dumbstruck to make sense of things. I suspected Alem knew about my smoking weed, although I had never done it in her presence. I was also getting angry, but right behind my exasperation, as usual, my guilt stood guard. *Alem went through an unspeakable ordeal. The least I can do is indulge her occasional outbursts of anger,* I reasoned.

"How could you? Drugs? *Ayee goud!* Is this why Emaye pawned the last of her jewellery to get you out of the country? Drugs? Drugs?" she repeated with a shrill voice.

"It's not a big deal, Alemiye," I said, as softly as I could, even though I knew she didn't take well to cajoling words anymore.

"Not a big deal? You want to pretend everything

is fine. You are somehow absolved of responsibility while others are rotting in prison or dead, is that it?" she continued.

"What are you talking about?" I said, rubbing my eyes and wiping sweat from my forehead.

"Oh I forgot. You are *Canadian*. You are beyond the petty skirmishes of savages in faraway lands," she said, dismissing imaginary people far behind me, the way one shoos rowdy kids away. Her mouth twitched with something like amusement and contempt.

I was at a complete loss. Had I smoked too much?

"Cut it out, Alem," I said and walked past her to the kitchen to get a glass of water.

She accosted me as I came back from the kitchen.

"This stuff is not as bad as cocaine or heroin or... sometimes I just need to relax. Forget everything and relax, do you understand?" I said.

"What do you have to forget? What have you *seen* that needs forgetting?" she said, her voice brimming with disdain.

I'd never hated anyone as I hated my sister at that instant. It was as if I was back home again and instead of my little sister, I was facing my father. But unlike Father's inflaming scorn, Alem's held in its centre something swift and cold, like a knife stab. I put down my glass of water on the coffee table and sat on the couch. I closed my eyes. When I opened them again, I saw Julie sitting beside me, looking at me with confusion.

"Sorry, Julie. Maybe you should go," I said with a sheepish smile.

"I'll call you later," I added as I closed the door behind her.

"You know what, Alem? I do what I can. I sponsored you. I send my share of money back home. What else do you want me to do?"

"It takes a man to do something," she grumbled and went into the kitchen.

I went to my bedroom and stood by my window. Kids were chasing each other around the slides and swings across from our building. I wondered again if there was more to Alem's anger than she led our parents and me to believe.

When we were kids, every Sunday morning after church, our parents would invite neighbours over for coffee. Father and the guests would sit on the veranda in their traditional white cotton garb, forming a crescent around Mother. They'd all sip thick black coffee out of tiny white-and-red porcelain cups while the aroma of *diffo* bread right out of a clay oven joined the scents of freshly cut grass and myrrh and frankincense smoke in the air. Some days, Mother would call Alem and me and hand us cups of coffee. We'd take a sip of the bitter brew and grimace. She'd then dump the rest of the liquid and study the patterns of coffee grounds on the bottom of the cups. With a solemn face, she'd interpret the criss-crossed maps of rivers, roads, and dwellings only she could see.

"You, Benny, you will become a wealthier and stronger lord than your father ever was," she'd say. "You, Alem, you will become a very successful teacher and marry a rich and honourable man."

Alem and I would argue about our assigned careers, at which point the adults would intervene with further speculations and teasing. Except for Father. He'd look from Alem to me and back with a pained smile on his face, certain that there was an irrevocable mix-up in the way his children turned out.

As I looked out my bedroom window into the jungle of high-rises, parking lots, and basketball courts, the world of kings, lords, and nobility that had died with Emperor Haile Selassie's deposition fifteen years earlier, in 1975, felt like the fantastic invention of a creative child. I felt a renewed rage bubble inside me. I missed my life before Alem. The loneliness and isolation were tough to bear, but at least back then I lived peacefully. I went to the kitchen, picked up an empty tomato can to use as an ashtray, and returned to my bed. I lit up a new joint and pressed play on my old tape player. Peter Tosh's "Johnny B. Goode" filled my senses.

"GIVE HER TIME. She's been through a lot," my friend Samson said when I told him of the incident the next day.

I was watching Samson throw one full bag after another into the garbage bin at the back of the Loblaws where we worked.

"I don't know," I said. "She's not the only one who's gone through hard times. Others did time too. Your brother for longer than she did. Eventually, you just have to move on, right?"

"Do you want some tea? It'll help you sober up. I can't believe you came to work high again. You need to stop this shit, man," he said.

We sat on the edge of the sidewalk in front of the grocery store's glass doors. The birds perched on the tall, naked trees across the deserted parking lot looked like dark, hard fruits against the streetlights.

He poured tea in his thermos lid and handed it to me. I watched the steam undulate in the cold October night.

"You know, growing up, I never could be the son my father wanted me to be," I said. "The more I tried, the more the concept eluded me. I was in trouble if I didn't do well in school. And if I spent more time than what he'd consider necessary in my room, he'd snatch whatever I'd be reading and shout: 'I am raising a son, for God's sake! Go outside and get into a fight or something.'"

"Same. My father never gave me time to ask what I did wrong before he charged at me with his belt," Samson said, laughing. "And I knew better than to ask questions."

"And regardless of what I had done, it always invariably turned to the Italians. 'Do you think we hid under our mothers' skirts like you?' he'd bellow. 'We fought them with whatever we could put our hands on. Like men.' I wanted so badly to remind him that the Emperor had run away to England when the Italians first invaded, but I didn't want to get punished for that too," I said. My anger was starting to wither.

"Oh, you definitely would have gotten the whipping of your life," Samson said. "The idea that Haile Selassie's move might have helped save the country didn't sit well with some of the more hardcore feudals such as your father and mine."

"Father was a completely different person with Alem though," I said. "Alem could refuse to eat or demand a different dish. She loved to play pranks on the old women in the neighbourhood. When Mother tried to chastise her, Alem would run to him and nobody could touch her. I hated her then."

The next day I told Alem I was going to move out. But before our lease was up, Father fell gravely ill so we were forced to stay in the apartment to save extra money for his hospital bills. We lived together for another two years, not as siblings but like an old couple who'd been angry at each other for so long they couldn't remember what had happened between them and no longer cared to fix it.

THE DAY ALEM finally divulged the secret that had been gnawing at her soul for over a decade, we were at our family home in Addis Ababa. It was in 1993, a few weeks after she and I had flown from Toronto for Father's funeral. A torrential rain was pounding on the tin roof of our house. Our mother's flower garden behind the screen of mist on the window was a blurry mix of reds and yellows bleeding into greens, reminiscent of water-colour applied on wet paper. I was thinking about our father.

"He was a war hero. And such a fair-minded and generous lord," Father's old friends had said. The withering hands and cloudy small eyes of recent pictures didn't belong to the unswerving man I remembered as my father.

"Do you remember how much Abaye loved playing his *krar*?" Alem said, brushing lint off my shoulder—Father's death had brought us closer together again. "One night, he was playing the instrument on the veranda. I sat with him as he finished a song. He sighed and, caressing the strings with his fingers, told me that, if it wasn't for his noble birth and the war against the Italian invaders, he would have pursued a career in music. Can you believe it?" she continued. "I guess he'd had a little too much to drink, because I could swear I saw tears in his eyes."

I searched her eyes for other things I might not have known or had forgotten about my father, about my past.

"He loved you, you know," she said with a distant smile.

I shrugged and looked away.

"He did. You are a lot more alike than you think," she said. "I wanted so badly for Abaye to think me worthy of his respect. I was so jealous of you."

"What are you talking about? It was always only about you," I said, not bothering to hide my old resentment.

"No. He let me do whatever I wanted when we were kids because, as a girl, he didn't expect me to amount to much. The best he could hope for me was that I'd marry someone like him. But you...he worried for you. He wanted rank and respectability for you but he didn't know how to express this. And deep down, in a way, I think he also envied you. He'd traded his dreams for honour as expected of him but you, you were never bound by tradition or duty. You always did whatever you wanted. You were always on the run, as though you were afraid someone might catch and nail you down to the ground."

I felt something inside me suddenly break open at the same time as I felt a tightening in my throat. I rushed to the veranda for some air.

The rain had stopped by then. Mother turned the cassette player in the living room on. I could hear an Orthodox Church *kidasse*, a choir of men and women clapping and chanting, leading the way to a climax of exultant drum beats that resonated throughout the house.

Alem came to sit beside me on the floor.

"I'm not going back. I'm staying here," she said after a few minutes.

To my silence, she added: "I'm staying, permanently."

Her words slapped my face raw.

"What? Why?"

"Death has a way of waking people up, I guess," she said, folding and unfolding a handkerchief our father had given her before she left for Canada.

"What about your job and the plans we made, remember? Save money and sponsor Mother. What are you going to do here?"

"You don't need me to sponsor Emaye." She stopped for a second. "You, you have your girlfriend. I know Elizabeth wants to settle down. You have your career. You love teaching and who knows, you might get tenure soon." She counted on her fingers the pieces that constituted my life in Canada.

"What about Joseph?" I said.

"It won't work," she said. "We're from two different worlds."

"People work things out, Alem. He loves you." I knew I had run out of ammunition.

She shook her head. "Besides, I don't want to be an assistant nurse for the rest of my life. Here, I can put my diploma to full use."

We stood in silence for a while.

"I also want to work on this new committee the government is setting up. It's tasked with tracking down members of the old regime," she whispered.

Two years earlier, in 1991, rebels from the North had toppled the Derg's seventeen-year-long reign and taken over the country. "Things are good now," everybody had been saying since, a slight wariness in their voices.

"The new government seems pretty reasonable," she said, reading my mind.

I thought of how the old government seemed reasonable at first too.

"Alem—"

"Those animals need to be apprehended," she interrupted me. "I need to do this," she said with a resolute voice.

I clenched my teeth.

"When I was in prison, there was another girl named Alem in my cell," she continued, studying the handkerchief in her hands, searching, it seemed, for an omen in the intricate embroidery of red flowers and green leaves.

I sighed. "How many times do I have to say it? You can't—"

She put her hand on my mouth and turned to look straight in front of her.

"One early morning, two guards came in our cell. All the women were still asleep. I was sitting by the wall facing the door, wondering if I would ever come out alive from that place—"

"No, seriously. You can't go on living your life in the past," I said.

She ignored me. "There was a lot of confusion in those days and the guards seemed edgier than usual," she said.

The rain began again. This time, it was light and silent and surrounded us like a protective screen.

"When one of the guards called out my name, I froze," she continued. "I couldn't speak or move. Everything around me became blurry. It felt as if I was having a vertigo attack. Then I heard my namesake cry and beg for her life, her voice distant as though I was under water. I was confused at first and then it hit me: she had not heard my last name called out." Alem stopped for a moment to swallow, her eyes still on the handkerchief in her trembling hands.

"I knew what I had to do but my body refused to act," she continued. "I felt myself disintegrating into the concrete floor. The guards dragged Alem out of the cell, screaming and fighting. I just sat there . . . I just sat there. She never came back." Alem sobbed, her back folded in. "A girl who had a mother and a father and three siblings waiting for her on the outside died because of me, Benny. I stole her life," Alem wailed, the ravages of her long-buried secret spilled on her face. "I'm a coward. I let her die," she continued after a while, still shaking against my body.

That night, I lay supine in my childhood bedroom, the cool night quiet save for Mother's phlegm-filled coughs coming from the next room and the occasional barks of stray dogs outside our gates. Snapshots of the twelve years Alem and I spent together in Toronto speckled my consciousness. I finally understood why she never talked about what had happened to her in prison, focusing instead, the very few times the subject came up, on generalities, on what had happened to everybody.

A WEEK LATER, on the way to Addis Ababa Airport, Alem and I sat in the back of Uncle Gueta's old Volkswagen with our mother. For the first time, I wished for Father's presence, to sit in that car beside the man I'd spent most of my life avoiding. I tried to imagine clasping his hand and reading love and care in his stern words but I could only picture his disapproving gaze.

Out the car window, people and beasts crossed streets at random points, and dilapidated blue and white taxis spewed charcoal-grey smoke in stalled traffic. I tried to imagine Alem wading through that mayhem, fending off catcalls from hustlers in crowded markets and our mother advising: "Ignore them, Alem. Otherwise, they'll know you're a foreigner and the pestering will get worse." Or navigating, with the urgency of an idealist, the snail-paced bureaucracy and general disorder of a government made up of guerilla fighters. "Be patient, my daughter, things are different here," our mother would counsel. I searched Alem's eyes for a sign. Would she be happy here? Would she find peace at last?

"I hope you'll have room for me in your new place," she said, her face peeling into a slow, reassuring smile. "You know, in case things don't work out here."

I arrived in Toronto at noon. After a twelve-hour sleep, I dragged myself to the living room. Alem's absence was palpable in the vapid air and dusty furniture. I went to the kitchen to get something to drink. On the fridge I noticed the calendar Alem used to catalogue her days. I started flipping through it. She had her work schedule at the hospital written in red, her evenings and weekends cleaning job in green. She'd also pencilled in major Ethiopian Orthodox holidays, birthdays, and anniversaries as a reminder to call home to wish our parents well. During all the years we lived together, Alem had kept her life on the other side of the world intact. I, on the other hand, couldn't remember the last time I'd picked up the phone to call our parents. Alem did the calling. She sent them the money I gave her. But she did more than that. She kept us grounded, linked to the other side of ourselves. This realization stirred in me a new kind of loneliness—the kind you feel when, having just arrived in a new city, you accidentally lose the only map of the place you had.

I went to the living room, stretched my limbs, and opened my fat suitcase to unearth from it a *gabi* that used to belong to Father. I lay on my couch wrapped in the thick fragrance of incense, spices, and home trapped in the cotton comforter. The intricate embroidery of royal blue and gold on the edges of the cream material distracted me from the suffocating silence of the apartment. I thought about my father and the fragmented memories of what we'd been to each other again. I thought about the years Alem had spent flagellating herself for having once succumbed to the most basic of human instinct: survival. And all the years I wasted running away from or reeling under the weight of her suffering. There was nothing I wanted more at that moment than to make up for lost time. I had missed my chance with Father, but I still had Mother and Alem. And for their sake and mine, I knew I had to start building a bridge. I needed to find a way to reify the home I left behind and to suture that world with the one I would wake up to daily.

Before I drifted off to sleep again, even though it was the middle of summer, I decided that I needed to purchase a new calendar.

children always stay

HELEN KNEW A THING OR TWO ABOUT LEAVING. When she was six, she and her parents left their home and everyone they knew in Addis Ababa in the middle of the night for a new life in Canada. Two years later, her father had walked out on her and her mother. Helen was relieved that the shouts, cursing, and cries that permeated her daily life had stopped. She didn't notice he had been gone any longer than usual until her mother told her he was never coming back. They were in the backyard, hanging clothes. Her mother washed their clothes by hand as a reminder of the things she'd lost: their big house in Addis Ababa with chauffeurs, gatekeepers, and maids; her expensive jewellery and clothes; her social standing as the wife of a powerful government official.

"I started out well, you know," her mom said. "I was only seventeen when I met him, but I already had a job in the city and a place of my own." She rested her hands on the clothesline, her head down as though she was talking to an invisible audience at her feet. "But that's what men do: take, take, and take. Your youth, your dreams. Your soul. Whatever they can until you're nothing but a hollow shell, dry and brittle like onion skin. Then they're gone. You better remember this." Her mother wagged her finger at her.

Helen's father had never taken anything from her, but Helen could tell from the fire in her mother's voice it was an important lesson. She nodded but her mother kept on staring at her for a long moment. There was something in her mother's eyes that Helen didn't have a name for. Something that made her little heart tighten.

Only on her deathbed, ten years later, did Helen's mother bring herself to speak about Helen's father or any other man again. Her mother had long ago discarded everything that belonged to Helen's father — his clothes, photos, books, favourite furniture — but something of him had persisted. It lived in the older woman's heavy sighs, in the dark circles around her eyes. And it hid in the shadows of her words and thoughts the way dust hides in dark corners of a house. Even when Helen hit puberty her mother couldn't bring herself to talk to her about sex or relationships with men. She'd just looked at her daughter's obstinately feminine body with furtive glances that spoke of fear and despair. It had made Helen feel tainted, repulsive.

Helen had run away from home when she turned seventeen and had been living with a friend for six months when she found out her mother was dying.

"Soon I'll be gone and you'll be truly alone," her mother said, reaching out for Helen's hand on the hospital bed. "But know this: men come and go," she continued, her voice raspy with lung cancer. "They talk a good talk about loyalty, morality, and family values, but when it comes down to it, they're the first ones to cheat, the first ones to break a vow, the first ones to desert their families."

Helen pulled the drab hospital curtains shut around them.

"Don't let them fool you. You hear? Don't waste your life on a man the way I did," her mother continued, as she struggled through a coughing fit.

Helen wiped the sweat on her mother's forehead.

"Men come and go," her mother said again. "Children, on the other hand, children always stay." She cleared her throat. "Even if they leave, they always come back. Like you did," she said, finally holding Helen's gaze, their eyes burning with all things unsaid.

When her mother passed away, Helen had nothing else left to lose. A distant uncle sold her mother's house and had her remains flown to Addis Ababa. When her mother's body was lowered into the ground, Helen's uncle and grandmother stood beside her, their hands pressing against hers. Helen didn't feel anything for them. She watched the ground swallow her mother. Her whole chest cavity had by then contracted itself around her heart and there was no room for anything or anybody else in it anymore.

THE FIRST TIME she walked out on a man, Helen was eighteen and travelling through California. She loved the uncertainty of foreign places, the anonymity that allowed her to reinvent herself, and to come and go without leaving a trace. He was a painter, very tall and wiry. He reminded her of the palm trees lining the streets of Venice Beach where he'd always lived. He had a serenity about him that made him look as though he could weather any storm. She found this reassuring, but it also made her despise him a little.

The day she left him, they had been seeing each other for three months. That morning, she'd turned on her side in his bed, away from him, and rested her eyes on one of his new paintings on the wall. Shades of brown, red, and green, a Black woman with an infant in her arms, mother and child blissfully smiling at each other.

"What do you think?" he asked, spooning her.

She turned her head and looked at him, almost surprised to find him there, even though they'd just had sex.

"Not bad," she said.

"That's it?"

"Well...it's a bit of a cliché, this depiction of Black womanhood, don't you think?"

He was silent.

"Let the words simmer in your mind before you speak," her mother used to tell her. But no matter how hard Helen tried, sometimes her thoughts just flew out of her mouth like projectiles.

"I mean, the colours are nice but..."

He hastily slid off the bed.

When she heard the shower running, she got up, almost stepping on the condom lying on the floor like a deflated balloon. There were variations of the same Black Madonna and baby on a few canvases stacked against the wall in the dining room. She felt queasy when she recognized her own features in the paintings.

She turned the coffee maker on and poured some milk to boil in a small pot. She turned the burner to low and stared at the milk.

The day before, they'd gone to Rodeo Drive, in Beverly Hills, just so they could pretend to be rich for an afternoon. They'd walked into an art gallery and stopped by one of Dalí's famous sculptures of a female figure with drawers set into her body. This one was called *Woman Aflame*. He'd walked around the small piece, enthralled.

"Dalí thought a woman's mystery was her true

beauty," he'd said, reading the inscription on the plaque at the sculpture's feet.

"Give me a break," Helen had muttered. It bothered her, this silencing of women, the false pretense. "What is it with you men? You just can't help it, can you?"

He'd looked at her with the innocence of a missionary. "What now?" he said. "How is complimenting a woman's beauty a bad thing?"

Helen had wondered what Dalí's wife, the strong-headed, outspoken Gala, must have had to say about her husband's views on feminine beauty.

"You used to be nice," he told her now, a towel around his waist, water droplets scintillating in his short afro. "These days all you do is criticize me or my work. What's going on?"

She skimmed her index finger over the milk in the pot. The milk skin stuck to her finger. She lifted it. It looked like a tiny closed umbrella in the space between their bodies. It reminded her of the used condom drying out by the bed. The ruins of lovemaking, bliss in past tense. She looked at the man in front of her and inscribed his features to memory.

As she drove out of Los Angeles surrounded by mountains that resembled camel humps, she thought of something she once read: *The nomadic blood aches for departures even when it's singing of arrivals.*

SHE HAD THIS recurring dream where she was a refugee woman crouched down beside her child in an old cart pulled by a dying donkey. Or perhaps she was the bloody child in rags and the older woman was her own mother, spine collapsing with each lift and drop of the wheels along the uneven path. All around them were dark skyscrapers, with brightly lit windows for eyes. They bent and contorted their metallic spines to prevent the refugees from leaving. Thousands of robotic eyes watching, threatening, while the sky above them slept the careless sleep of a god. These dreams were always the harbinger of another departure, another leap toward the unknown.

THE NEXT MAN she left, she'd met while teaching ESL at an elementary school in Osaka. She found a bit of familiarity in the manners of the Japanese she talked to outside of work—shopkeepers, waiters, and random strangers. The way they bowed their heads to greet her, the way they stretched both arms to hand her the merchandise she'd bought or how they received their payment with the same humble gestures—it all reminded her of the manners she was brought up on as a child, long since replaced with Western mores.

He was short and solidly built and had been living in Osaka for five years. He looked as if he could keep her steady against the shifting of the ground or the anger in the winds.

The day she decided to leave him, they were in Tokyo for a few days. That evening, she'd held on to his arm as they walked among hundreds of pedestrians in Akihabara district, gleefully basking in the clement fall weather, her senses saturated with the reds, blues, yellows, and pinks of the neon lights flashing off giant boards advertising manga characters, video games, and other electronics. He suggested they check out one of the gaming centres. There was an urgency and child-like excitement on his face that demanded acquiescence. They walked up one escalator after another, past aisle upon aisle of arcades and VR stations. On the top floor, there were two white-and-pink stations set up in a secluded corner, as if put there as an afterthought, to cater to female gamers' interests.

"No wonder no one is using them. Look how boring these stations are," she said to him, raising her voice to be heard above the ambient noise.

He shrugged. He was reading the instructions on one of the other stations. "I want to try this one. Do you mind?" he said, already adjusting the seat in front of the monitor.

He'd started the game without waiting for her answer. She bit her lip. A few teenage girls watched their boyfriends play with the learned patience of older women. Others, less resigned, pulled on the boys' arms trying to distract them from the games. Even though she was at least five years older than these girls, she recognized herself in them. And despite his age, her boyfriend also resembled all the other young men in the room, their unblinking eyes glued on their screens, their minds in a surreal world far away from the dingy room that their bodies — and those of the women waiting for them — occupied. She felt her chest tighten. *This is just a video game,* she told herself, *a momentary escape from reality,* but there was something about being the one left behind, the one waiting, that bothered her deeply.

Before they headed out to Ebisu district where they'd booked a room for the night, he'd suggested they stop at a famous mom-and-pop ramen joint that had been run by the same couple for over thirty years. Plastic samples of various bowls of ramen were displayed behind the glass wall under the cash register. The noodles, meats, *naruto,* and other condiments were all perfectly sculpted and painted to imitate the real things. Something of an art form in Japan, she would later learn.

"I guess having pictures of the damn things in a menu was not good enough," she said.

"Why are you salty today? This is awesome," he said.

They ordered their food and sat in a quiet corner, wearing oversized paper bibs. He flipped through TripAdvisor's suggestions of must-see places in Tokyo, reading aloud for her benefit. She followed the husband and wife duo in the open kitchen behind the cash register as they bent and twisted their bodies around each other in the narrow space, mesmerized by their perfect timing as they assembled steaming bowls of ramen and placed them on the counter for the server to pick up. She wondered how long it had taken them to fine tune this daily dance, the sacrifices required to achieve such harmony, whose habits and choices had prevailed and who'd had to compromise. And what would happen if one of them suddenly picked up and left? She looked at her boyfriend again and the ridiculous bib around his neck. She foresaw herself fading away into his world. She felt that familiar tightening, but in her throat this time. She focused on all the little things that bothered her about him. The way he insisted she look him in the eye when they had sex, his heavy grunts, the way his sweat smelled sour afterward. She started to rid herself of these memories. She started to let go of him.

She spent the night alone in a tiny room in a cheap hotel that brought to mind a sepulcher but she thought of it as a space travel pod instead. She dreamed of stars, of the infinitely empty space between them. Of the limitless possibilities they promised.

THEN THERE WERE relationships that ended before they even began, such as the one she had with an old high school crush. He'd invited her to visit him in Dubai after they'd seen each other at an old classmate's wedding. As she waited for him to pick her up at the airport, she'd watched women dressed all in black scurrying behind men all in white. The men's gait was purposeful, their gaze assured and outward focused; the women's bodies folded onto themselves, their eyes lowered. She wondered what these women thought or spoke about when they were alone or with other women. Would they trade places with her?

When he picked her up, she told him about this to break the ice.

"Things aren't the same in these parts of the world," he said. He had the tone of someone warning an inexperienced, Western tourist.

She swallowed her irritation. She'd never travelled this far for the sole purpose of being with a man before so she'd hoped things would be different. She couldn't quite fathom what *different* meant for her, but she was turning thirty and felt it was time to figure that out.

They drove past hundreds of skyscrapers, wide highways, and familiar brands on billboards. The sky was heavy with manufactured rain.

"I guess this is what oil buys," she said, making a sweeping gesture at the landscape unfolding around her.

"Dubai doesn't produce oil anymore, but Abu Dhabi still does," he said, confidently.

She was too tired and jetlagged to explain herself. She bit her lip.

They drove by the marina, the water sparkling with the lights wrapped around the palm trees lining the bay.

"Unlike in North America, here they stay lit all year long," he told her, his face beaming as if he had something to do with the wealth that made this possible.

As she chewed on fettuccine alfredo that tasted of rancid butter and old cheese, she watched him. They were in a restaurant lounge overlooking the water, a room packed with people sipping on alcohol and smoking shisha. House music blasted out of huge speakers at each corner of the room — she felt it pulsating in her head as though it were spilling out from within her throbbing blood vessels. His body twitched with boisterous excitement as he bobbed his head to the beat. He greeted nearby people as if he owned the place. It made him look too young and eager. Her spine stiffened against the thinly veiled proprietary rights he displayed as he introduced her to the other expats and against the unsubtle assent of men appraising merchandise. It made her want to wipe the glee off their faces, made her want to take something from him.

By the time he unlocked the door to his apartment, she felt her fingertips throb with the need to grab and claw. Her teeth ached to bite and tear through flesh and bone. She instructed him not to turn the lights on. They ripped each other's clothes off in the dark. She straddled him. He was a blank canvas. He was any man and no one at all. She was all flesh and pleasure. She took all he had on offer and by the time they were done, only her body was still in the room. She left while he was in the kitchen making her tea.

To make most of the situation, she signed up for a desert safari. As the driver of the four-wheel drive sped along immaculate highways out of the city, Helen took in the treacherous desert surrounding them, the mangled tires melting in the sun. She breathed in the ungodly heat. She revelled in the vastness and beauty of the desolate land, the dunes rising and falling into the horizon. She thought of the peace and silence ahead.

SHE DATED OTHER, more sophisticated men. Men who'd eventually made her feel like a shipwrecked sailor: small and disoriented. And some of them left her. But she didn't allow herself to think about these men often. Whenever she felt herself falling for a man, she went to visit her mother's grave in Addis Ababa. She could always count on her mother to remind her what it cost to love.

A few months after one of those visits, she met another man. She'd stayed in Addis Ababa because a cousin, who'd heard about her work in international development, had offered her a contract as an economic advisor at an NGO based in the city. When she wasn't wading through the murky waters of foreign aid and its often nefarious effects on the people it was supposed to help, she surrendered herself to the ebbs and flows of her grandmother's daily life, which included old friends, cousins, neighbours, and strangers. No matter how many times she came back, it always felt odd to be surrounded by so many people who looked like her. She stared at them as if they were all distant relatives she was supposed to remember.

He was the same age and almost the same height as her. He spoke her mother tongue and shared her love for travel. *"Qui se ressemble, s'assemble,"* he told her in his heavily accented French.

He took to picking her up from her grandmother's house. As they drove around the crowded city in his old Mercedes-Benz, he'd point at important landmarks and tell her about their historical significance: Menelik II and the Lion of Judah statues, Tewodros Square, Africa Hall, the Yekatit 12 monument. Sometimes, he'd give her a broad and unreserved smile that made her feel as if they'd always known each other. And other times, she'd watch him stare into the distance, lost in his thoughts, and she'd think of final departures, of loss. But eventually, as he passionately related their common history to her, she started to feel his pride (and sometimes his anger) as her own. Where she grew up, Black heroes were hard to come by, let alone female ones, so she especially enjoyed hearing him tell Empress Taytu's story. Empress Taytu had not only seen through the Italians' ruse to have her husband, Emperor Menelik II, sign a treaty that would have made Ethiopia an Italian protectorate in the late nineteenth century, but she'd also led her own army to the Battle of Adwa to deal the Italians one of the most humiliating defeats suffered by European colonizers anywhere in the world. Then one day, Helen found herself daydreaming about a daughter she'd name after Empress Taytu.

The day she really felt herself falling for him, they were at the National Museum. She'd found it hard to resist the idea that they fit together, that they were part of each other as much as they were part of the historical figures they were learning about. Helen had decided to visit her mother's grave after he dropped her off, but her grandmother was waiting outside for them and had invited him in for lunch.

After lunch, he and Helen sat on a rock pile by the compound wall facing her grandmother, their arms touching a little. Helen was fanning the charcoal stove on top of which her grandmother had placed a deep pot. The old woman cut big chunks from the block of milk-white butter she'd had the maid buy at the market and brought the pieces to her nose to test their freshness before she dropped them in the pot she'd lined with a bed of garlic, ginger, and *koseret* and other spices she'd just roasted and ground. The butter slowly turned greenish yellow as it melted into the fenugreek, *beso bela*, and *korarima*. With a big wooden spoon, her grandmother gently pushed chunks of still-solid butter floating in the liquid against the wall of the pot to speed their melting. As she did these things, the old woman hummed a song. Its slow, heart-wrenching melancholy filled Helen's chest with joy and sorrow for things she couldn't name. There was stillness in the air and in her grandmother's gentle voice that made Helen's breathing easier.

"What are you singing?" Helen asked. "It sounds so familiar."

"It's 'Tizita.' It's the longing and memory connecting you to me, you to him, and to all the ones that came before us. And those that will come after us too," she said. There was a hint of Helen's mother's eyes in the way the old woman looked at her.

The scent of clarified butter took hold of Helen's senses. She thought about her mother's funeral. Her rigid, cold body inside the ornate casket. She imagined her mother's heart coming alive with each shovel-full of earth thrown at it. She pictured the body warming up, loosening, and growing tendrils to latch onto the casket's walls, then breaking through the box. She imagined the tendrils transformed into umbilical cords, her mom reaching out to the soil of her birth like a fetus to its mother. She pictured her mother's features creasing into a smile as her body fed itself back to life, then folded into the warm embrace of her ancestors.

"Stop fanning the fire, love," her grandmother instructed. "You don't want the butter to burn."

For a moment, Helen couldn't remember a time before that second in her grandmother's backyard, but she knew in her bones, something had led her to that instant. She no longer felt shipwrecked, adrift, or seasick. She stood on firm ground.

She pushed her thigh against his. She longed to be alone with him and her desires again: to touch him, kiss him, to feel him move inside her, to see in his eyes what she felt, to break through the constraining weight on her chest, to let her heart find its own beat.

Later on, as he made love to her, she was, for a moment, distracted by the mixture of orange peel and roasted coffee scent on his fingers. It had the tang of something burnt. It reminded her of the smell of cigarette smoke on an old lover's hands. Then she remembered her mother's words: *Men come and go but children always stay.*

"We don't need this," she said to him, and reached down for the condom.

She took in his surprise, watched it turn into delight. She felt nostalgic almost. She wrapped her legs tighter around his waist and synced her rhythm to his. She closed her eyes and focused her thoughts on a daughter she would name Taytu.

learning to meditate

I MET HIM ON A FRIDAY EVENING. I WAS IN FRONT OF the building where I worked, pretending to be waiting for someone. In reality, I was avoiding going home.

"Are you alright? You look troubled," he said. With his thick, white beard and watery, brown eyes, he was a perfect picture of wisdom and solicitude.

I must have stared at him blankly. He looked me straight in the eye as if he'd always known me, as if he knew I'd lost my way, and asked: "Would you care to go somewhere and talk?"

I didn't have the clarity of mind to accept or decline his invitation, so I stood there thinking about the empty apartment that still harboured my boyfriend's shadows a month after he'd left me. I pictured myself entering its dark mouth, mindlessly turning on one light after another, feeding the microwave a frozen dinner from a pile in the freezer, and downing one mug-full of expensive wine after another as I flipped through glossy magazines, searching for myself in them.

"Follow me," he said, and I followed him past tall glass and chrome buildings glimmering in the rain, past men and women in business suits and no-nonsense faces, scurrying to catch their buses home, past war and freedom statues overseeing an elaborate traffic system.

He pointed at a pub called Yesterday's. I took that as a sign.

Funny how sudden the time between lost and found.

MY FATHER WAS a silent stranger I carried inside. He never had time for PTA meetings, his children's birthdays, or his wife's concerns. Whenever he deigned to speak to us, it was to remind us of the people who were dying in his home country's civil war, of his younger brother who'd suffocated in a metal barrel while hiding from government soldiers, or of his obligations to the Resistance. What I wished to forget was how the air always felt thinner, harder to breathe when he was around; how I'd resigned myself to the inevitability of hearing my mother's stifled cries as she rushed down the corridor past my bedroom to the bathroom late at night; or how hot, fragrant tea trembled in its cup as she set the table for breakfast the next day.

HE ORDERED PINTS of Alexander Keith's for us.

"It breaks my heart to see such a beautiful, young *sistah* looking so beaten down," he said.

I wanted to tell him I wasn't as young as he probably thought (I looked eight to ten years younger than my real age, which was thirty), but I didn't want to interrupt him.

"I know things," he continued, smoothing his beard with thick fingers. "Whatever you're going through, I've been through it. Probably many times over."

I watched the frothy head of foam on my beer slowly deflate before I took a good gulp and wiped my mouth with my thumb.

"You are so beautiful," he said again.

There was something unsettling and yet familiar in the way he looked at me, but I felt too tired and my mind was too foggy to try to decipher its meaning.

He loosened his gaze and cleared his throat. "I was married for twenty-five years. My wife died last year," he said, his eyes now on his half-empty glass.

"I'm sorry," I said.

He shook his head. "That's alright. That's life."

I noticed the fraying collar of his windbreaker, the clean but thin button-down shirt underneath. I infused my imagining of his life with financial hardship, heartache, and loneliness. I saw a man of dignified bearing who, despite it all, had come to grips with life's shortcomings. It made me feel sorry for him. And it made me feel closer to him.

"See, we are all guests in this world. This is not our home. We're here to learn and grow, and we're only given one chance," he said. "So we shouldn't squander it."

"I read an article not long ago that postulated we might all be simulations run by a highly advanced civilization," I said.

His brow furrowed. He narrowed his eyes as if he were trying to make out my features from a distance.

"You know, like characters in video games," I continued.

What I really wanted to tell him was that my one chance at a good life might have been destroyed the day I first witnessed my father's violence break my mother into a bundle of howling sounds and tears as though she'd regressed into infancy. That remembering this made me wish I could cry into his shoulder the way I used to with my grandfather, when I was little and he was still alive.

He shook his head. "I don't know anything about that . . . And young lady, you shouldn't buy into that white folk nonsense either," he said, shaking his hand in front of me.

His tone betrayed the nature of a man who didn't take well to contradiction.

I nodded. I didn't care that his assertion was ridiculous. In fact, I welcomed it — not only because my boyfriend was the one who'd read the article and this man's dismissal therefore was a negation of everything that he stood for, but also because it had been so long since I'd had a conversation with someone who looked like me that his rebuttal was in itself, an acknowledgement. A reminder of who I'd been before I moved to the city, before my boyfriend made me believe I could change if I really wanted to, and before I became a hollow vessel instead.

He took a big gulp of his drink. "Anyway, things might look a little overwhelming right now, but the world is out there waiting for you. You just need someone to help you find a path through the fog."

I wanted to disappear into the depth of his reassuring baritone. I nodded again.

My grandmother could read lifelines in wet coffee grains. She told tales of switchbacks and backroads ahead, of beguiling serpents hunting by day or by night, but also of guardian angels sprinkled here and there like light posts on dark country roads.

Funny how deeply etched, how immediate, is the need to find a trail home.

MY MOTHER WAS fond of telling people that I'd been a precocious and responsible child. "Even as a toddler, she never complained or cried in front of strangers," she'd say as she discreetly pressed her hand flat on my back to remind me to bend like a lady when I served her guests refreshments. She told stories of how she could always reason with me or confide her heartaches and pains in me the way she would with a sister. Or how, when visiting family friends gave me money to buy treats or toys, I used to ask to spend it on school supplies instead.

I remembered things differently. By the time I was four or five years old, before I could articulate shame, I knew it was shameful to touch my private parts; I knew to sit with my legs closed tight together, and to pull at the hem of my skirt. By the time I was seven, before I could grasp the mechanism of sex and reproduction, I knew the world could hurt me in a way that my brother could never be hurt, that I was prey and that, if something happened to me, it would be my fault. So when my gym teacher in grade three made it a habit to touch me in ways I knew were inappropriate, I couldn't tell anyone, especially not my mother. I couldn't let her down. And later on, when other men hurt me, I'd tell myself it was only my body they broke, that they couldn't touch me where it mattered. I couldn't let myself down.

HE SIGNALLED THE waiter for two more pints. I thought of refusing his offer but I didn't want to look disagreeable.

A couple sitting across from us pulled their chairs closer together around a small table.

The first few months after we started dating, my boyfriend and I sat with our knees touching under the table too or, if we were assigned a booth, we sat on the same side, our thighs and legs stitched together. We ate from each other's fingers, each other's mouths. We memorized each other's words and mannerisms. When he moved inside me, I made noises to please him. *It will do for now*, I told myself to conceal the possibility that I might never feel what other women felt.

"So tell me. Is it about a boy?" he asked, following my eyes.

"No," I said a little too quickly.

"You live with your parents?"

"No, I have my own place."

"An independent woman. I respect that," he said. "But it's tough out there when you're alone, isn't it? Though maybe not for one as fine as you. You must have many suitors," he said with eyes that spoke of experience.

"No, not really," I said.

"A woman is never complete without a husband and children," he said and paused. "But it has to be the right kind of man. Don't get me wrong, a man needs a good woman by his side too. But young men these days..." He pursed his lips and shook his head emphatically. He downed the rest of his beer and continued: "Young men these days, they're not mature enough, not man enough, to know what well-grounded and intelligent young women like you need."

There was an intrusive quality to his almost shy smile. I felt a knot tighten somewhere deep in my stomach. I took a long swig of my drink and turned my thoughts to memories of my boyfriend's generous smile, the kind that made you think you're in on whatever made him grin or laugh. It took me over a year to see the blind optimism behind that bright smile. To him, life was as simple and straightforward as the video games he loved to play: a succession of problems to be solved, quests and goals to be achieved. He was the knight out saving the damsel in distress, the elite commander defending Earth against alien races, the sharpshooter fighting evil lurking in dark, urban dwellings. He couldn't fathom that life could beat you down to a pulp, break you into multitudes of irreconcilable fragments that no amount of effort or will could mend.

"HE WASN'T ALWAYS like this," my mother would say when I asked why Father was always angry. When social workers or the police urged her to press charges against him, she would just nod until they left. "What would people say? The shame," she'd say to me once we were alone. Or she'd shake her head and groan: "What do these people know about us? How could they understand? We can't put him in jail after all he's been through, okay?"

I would nod, not to appease her, but because I knew from the news on TV that sometimes men who were sent to prison for hurting their wives or girlfriends would return to kill them when they got out.

When I turned eleven, my mother told me I'd become someone's wife someday and if I was lucky, a mother to good children. "In the meantime," she said, "men will try to take advantage of you." So I needed to learn to protect myself until the right man came along.

I already knew what men wanted from me, of course. I'd felt the bone-chilling gaze of my gym teacher's lust on me, the laboured breaths that coat the skin like grime. But my mother couldn't tell me how to discern the *right* man from the others, so I gravitated toward those who showed the most persistence, the ones who seemed to know they had a right to my body. Some of these men didn't ask for my consent. And I didn't stop them. There was an order to things, a silent acquiescence that romance and propriety demanded of me. But sometimes, there was also a thrill in knowing that these men full of want and anger desired *me*.

"DO YOU PRACTISE meditation?" the man asked. His voice rose when he said this, as though he'd just had an epiphany.

I shook my head.

"You should try it," he said. "Meditation is self-knowledge. It'll bring you inner strength, peace, and joy."

He talked about galactic formations and cosmic vibrations, of the power of love to enlighten us and bring us closer together, of one day returning to our rightful place among the stars.

I ached to believe I could attain all the things this man was promising meditation would bring me.

Outside, the moon was a disc of soft cream against the black sky, a porthole into another world. I imagined myself freed of the doubts and sense of failure gnawing at my bones.

"I'm certified to teach it. If you wish, I could teach you," he said, watching me intently.

"Maybe," I said and smiled.

Funny how readily the crust of dead skin splits open under the spell of an old man's tale of the circle of life.

MY BOYFRIEND'S LOVE felt good and it felt portentous, like floating in deep waters. Some days, he'd grab and pull me to him and I'd feel my skin hum with the need and love for him. Other times, his gaze would feel suspect, as if it wasn't me he was looking at but a fantasy he'd conjured up, and his softest touch would hurt like a lick of fire. *Let it go, he's good to you, move on,* I'd tell myself at the first intimations of a storm brewing inside, but it would be in vain. I'd find a million little ways to attack him for having failed to see me as I was. I'd flirt with strangers or make fun of his sheltered, middle-class upbringing in front of his friends. I'd accuse him of pitying me, anything to provoke him, to find a line to cross, to unfurl the violence I assumed lived coiled inside him.

"Let's see the real you," I'd encourage him. "Let's see what you've got."

Sometimes he'd ask: "You're testing me, aren't you? Trying to push me away. See how much I can take?" And he'd hold me tight in his arms until I softened into a silent cry.

Other times, his face would turn white for a second before he'd kick the nearest object out of his way, lurch at me, and with a firm grip on my arms force me to stand still in place, his beautiful face flush with outrage.

"There it is. Let it out," I'd tell him and my heart would thump with the frenzy of imminent victory. He'd quickly let go and stare at me with horrified eyes for a while, then pack up a few of his things and disappear for days until I begged him to come back.

"Don't be so fatalistic, baby," he would say when we made up after a week or two spent apart. "You can't let what happened between your dad and mom define you. Or us."

I'd want to tell him there was more he didn't know about me, but there would be so much conviction in his voice that I'd choose instead to believe it was possible to let go of the past. I'd daydream about reinventing myself, about new beginnings and second chances.

But even after two years together, I'd still sometimes wake in the middle of the night feeling adrift, dislocated in body and mind. Some nights, he would gently pull me to his side of the bed, fold his arm around me, and kiss me in the nape of my neck before falling back into deep sleep. I'd lay there, eyes wide open, willing the memory of that kiss to burn through my skin, my flesh and bones, and settle in my heart. Other times, I'd watch him sleep and wish I could penetrate his dreams so that I could find a new language for us in them. But he'd look so peaceful, so far away, I'd know he could never really see me as I was. And it would dawn on me again that what he offered me — a love free of fear and pain, and a life built on consent, trust, and compromise — would always be beyond my grasp too.

WE SAT IN silence for a while. The pub was busier and noisier than when we'd first arrived. Outside, the rain had started again. It looked as though millions of rubies and emeralds were crashing against the slick asphalt and the cars whooshing by. I quietly tapped my feet to a pop song playing in the background.

"Tell you what," he said. "Why don't we go to my place? It's only a few blocks away. I have scented candles.

Red ones and cream-coloured ones." He looked past me for a moment, trying to remember if he had the colours right. "What do you say?" he continued before I had time to respond, leaning closer to me across the table.

He covered my hand with his.

There was suddenly something unhinged in the way he looked at me. I recognized the slippery sharpness of avowed lust in his eyes.

My breath caught in my throat. I stared at his hand as he gently wrapped it around my wrist. A wild cat's jaws clasping a child's bones.

"Or, if you prefer, we can pick up the candles and go to your place," he said, patting my hand before he let go.

He stretched one arm across his torso.

I caught a glimpse of the contours of a burly arm under his windbreaker. The power in his shoulders, in his big hands.

Funny how thin the line between safety and fear, how abrupt the shift in vision.

"THE HEART NEVER FORGETS," my mother used to say, "but you have to be as patient and light as water. That's the only way for a woman." And some days, she'd look at me with a smile that hinted at hope and say: "There is a secret power to water, you know, the kind of strength that carves fissures in mountains and turns stone to mud."

I'd search for signs of weariness in my father's hard stare to corroborate my mother's teachings. But in the end, my mother was the one who'd lost the battle. I learned then that the erosion of the soul, like that of the land, is slow coming. By the time I left home, my mother had evaporated into a whisper.

I ORDERED ANOTHER pint and examined the skin on my wrist and hand where he'd touched me, expecting it to change colour or texture.

I thought about other men. Men I'd known before I'd met my boyfriend. Rich, white men leaning close to me at formal parties or work-related events and whispering the things they'd buy me if I was willing to spend some time alone with them. Or middle-aged men with thick accents and heavy gold necklaces who kept their wives and daughters on a tight leash but openly ogled dark-skinned girls like me. There were Black men too. And yet it shocked me that I didn't see it coming this time, that I was so wrapped up in my own misery that I'd chosen to ignore the signs. A gush of self-loathing and defeat filled my throat. That's when I finally saw it. The anger, the want just below the surface of his wet smile. I knew why this man approached me. And why I'd followed him to the pub. This man and I knew each other the way my boyfriend and I couldn't. He was a piece of my past reclaiming me.

"Okay," I said.

I heard my voice, I recognized myself sitting across from him but felt disconnected from my thoughts and feelings.

A subtle look of surprise flashed across his face. "Let me go settle the bill then," he said and quickly went to the bar.

I watched the rain trickle down the window. I felt the emptiness inside pushing into my ribcage.

I remembered how even my ever-cheerful boyfriend had eventually grown weary. "I can't do this anymore," he'd said. "You need professional help." As he spoke, I picked at dried drops of food on the kitchen counter. He rubbed the back of his neck and with a forced enthusiasm that made me wish I could disappear into a circle of darkness in the ground, he added: "Maybe it's just hard to overcome things on your own, sometimes."

I looked at the man as he walked back from the bar. His steps were light, his face lit with anticipation.

"Ready?" he said, a youthful urgency to his voice.

I imagined following him past a busy street corner or two, past boisterous businessmen waiting for cabs, their ties loose around their necks, their bellies round and faces flushed with the aftermath of one-too-many Happy Hour specials; past dark, residential streets where wet, leafless vines crawled up the blood-red brick walls of expensive houses like thousands of leeches feeding. I pictured myself following him into a

shabby, short apartment building, then up a dark stair-
case, shadows zigzagging on the dimly lit wall like the
snakes in my grandmother's coffee grains. I imagined
thinking about my boyfriend for a moment, then about
my mother, about shame that settles in the blood and
memories that confine like a straightjacket before I let
myself disintegrate into nothingness. I found solace in
these thoughts, a certain kind of homecoming. I felt
the release of tension in my bones.

Funny how dangerously easy it is to sink back into
the darkness within.

you made me do this

MARIAM TIGHTENED HER HIJAB AND TUCKED ITS end under her chin for the hundredth time that day. Every time a woman pressed herself against Mariam's shoulders to express her condolences, the flimsy polyester fabric came undone, sliding off her thin, grey-streaked hair. But Mariam was too tired to go upstairs to her bedroom to get a better scarf or to ask someone for a pin to secure the one she was wearing.

Her friend Asma, whose loud weeping had just started to subside into snuffles, dried her eyes with her own shawl and asked: "Do the police have any leads?"

That's another thing Mariam was tired of already: people asking if the police were any closer to finding the man who'd killed her son, Ismail, two days earlier. She shook her head, shifted around on the couch she shared with Asma, then discreetly slid her body to the end of the seat.

Asma adjusted the pillows behind Mariam's back to ease the sciatica she knew her friend suffered from.

"I'm fine," Mariam murmured, trying to keep her tone from betraying her annoyance — she didn't want to be waited upon. She was not a bride or a new mother to be pampered. If anything, she wished to be left alone. She looked at her watch: three hours before her daughter's flight from Vancouver would land at the Ottawa International Airport. Without Mona, she felt under siege in her own home.

After their initial loud keening, those of her friends who knew Ismail well huddled around her, bowed down with grief. The ones who had teenage sons around Ismail's age struggled with their growing fear of a city that seemed to be more and more determined every day to devour their children like an angry, voracious sea. Others sat still, lost in their own past, slowly peeling scabs off old pains, reviving with silent tears and occasional sighs the memories of those they'd long laid to rest.

Mariam had been in these women's shoes many times before. She had sat with them in their time of mourning. She had shared their tears, consoled them with the appropriate words, recited the right *surahs* to remind them of the impenetrability of God's plans and of the special place in Heaven reserved for the faithful. That's what friends do for each other and what a community does for its members. But she never believed such a calamity would strike *her* home. Not really. And losing one's child, she realized now, was not only about loss and separation but also about defeat, a crushing sense of failure that no words or tears could ever absolve.

She heard the clatter of dishes as three or four of her friends cleared the dining table where the foods that visitors had brought—*injera*, rice, and bowls of various sauces—had been set up for lunch. A few kids criss-crossed her field of vision as they ran up and down the stairs. When someone opened the door to the basement, the voices of the men gathered there around her husband, Ahmed, rose to the main floor and commingled with those of the women and children. Mariam saw and heard these things peripherally, like being aware of the muddled noise while making her way through a busy market. In a way, that was what she'd been doing since she'd learned about her son's death: wading through the jumbled memories of her life, sifting for clues, for a reason why Allah had rescued her from certain death eighteen years earlier, brought her to this cold country, and gave her a son just to take him away so quickly.

When the police officers came to her door two days earlier, Mariam had expected them to say they were looking for her son for questioning—it seemed as though the police were always trailing young men like

Ismail in this neighbourhood—or even to arrest him the way they had a few months earlier, when he was detained for a week in relation to a murder that took place a few blocks away. This time, she was ready to stand up for her son, to tell the officers to stop harassing the poor boy. But when they told her of Ismail's death, she was stunned into silence. She'd looked directly into the clear eyes of the officer who'd said the word *dead*, expecting to find a rebuttal. But there was nothing in them except maybe a slight fatigue. She'd felt unsteady on her feet. She'd struggled to breathe, to say something, then simply collapsed. When she came to, she was in her bed. A police officer was looking down at her. She heard women's cries somewhere close by. She closed her eyes and opened them again.

"Are you okay, ma'am?" the police officer asked.

She saw her husband's bloodshot eyes at the foot of the bed. She nodded and closed her own eyes again.

As the fact of her son's death surged through her mind, it brought with it a new awareness: she knew why her son was killed. She recognized her hand in it. She remembered how agitated and reclusive Ismail had become after he was released from jail, the accusation that burned bright in his eyes whenever he deigned to look at her. She'd felt too triumphant for having saved him from imprisonment to consider the dangers she'd exposed him to.

This realization now sat at the centre of her heartbreak like a big block of ice slowly melting into her bloodstream, eroding her body from the inside out. She wished she had not recovered consciousness at all. Or that she had died that time eighteen years earlier — seven months before Ismail's birth — when she'd said her *shahada* on that unforgiving, barren land on the border between Eritrea and Sudan and had closed her eyes on the world. She wished to go back to that moment so she could close her eyes but for good this time. But death doesn't come so easily to those who seek it.

MARIAM FELT A cold draft as a tall, thin man in a leather jacket closed the front door. For a second her heart leaped across the room; she thought the man was Ismail.

"*Assalam Aleykum*," said Hamza, her husband's friend, as he took his shoes off at the door, his voice devoid of its usual gaiety.

"*Aleykum Assalam. Tefedal*," the women in the kitchen replied with equally restrained voices.

Mariam watched Hamza make his way past the women and children to the living room before she got up to greet him.

"I'm so sorry, *haftey*. I was away for work. I just heard today," Hamza said, his right palm on his chest, his body bent slightly in reverence.

"Thank you, Hamza. I know."

"*Ayee!* This is such a painful loss to all of us. He was such a good boy. So polite, respectful of his elders. Just like a son to Fatima and me."

"I know, I know. Thank you, Hamza."

"May Allah grant you patience and fortitude in this time of trial, my sister," Hamza said.

"Thank you, brother. The men are downstairs," she said, averting her eyes from him.

This is another thing she was tired of: people describing her son to her as if he weren't the boy she gave birth to, the boy she'd nursed for two full years. The baby smell in the folds of his chubby little neck and arms that she used to love so much. The way it made her feel, the first time his little body wobbled on the snow, weighed down by the pink snowsuit and matching winter boots she'd bought him from Zellers — she didn't yet know that in Canada, pink was for girls. His boundless energy, his easy laughter, his hunger for stories. When he was a toddler, only her stories could keep him seated long enough to be fed. But by the time he was in preschool, he had his own stories to recount — tales of good guys and bad guys, cops and robbers, sirens and chases, gunshots and surrenders, all picked up from other kids in the neighbourhood. She didn't make much of this back then. Boys got excited over toy trucks and firefighters, too. Later on, she'd wondered if she should have paid closer attention, if Ismail's interest in these kinds of stories presaged his future failings. But children grow up so fast. She didn't see any of it coming until one day, when he turned fourteen, she noticed he had shot up like wild grass to tower over her and his father and suddenly, trying to talk or beat sense into him had become harder than trying to infuse life into a brick wall.

WHEN SHE FIRST followed her husband into exile, she knew the journey across the border into Sudan would be arduous. That's why she'd left Mona, who was two years old at the time, with her own parents in Asmara. But only when, four days into the trek, they ran out of water did she realize the trip would prove to be dangerous even for a healthy young woman such as herself. Two days later when the encouraging smiles on Ahmed's face turned to a look of resignation and maybe even of irritation, she knew her end was near. She didn't want to see her shame in his eyes so she'd squinted one more time for a sign of hope past the shimmering, arid landscape in front of her, then scanned the mountains for government soldiers and rebels before she'd let her body fall to the ground.

"Leave me be," she'd said. "It won't be long."

But Ahmed and their guide had picked her up and carried her for a while until she was able to walk on her own again. Eventually — she learned this later, in Khartoum — her eyes had rolled back, her body flailing for a second before she'd collapsed. The men had covered her body with her shawl, stretching and weighing the ends of the dirty cotton cloth down with rocks. They'd scooped sand with their hands and spread it on her body. Then, after reciting a quick prayer, Ahmed had touched her face one more time before he followed the guide's agile steps.

What she remembered later were the hallucinations she'd had as she waited for death to come. First, the wind blew hot sand the colour of gold, copper, and silver around her. Then came the children's cheerful voices. She heard Mona's laughter. She heard the rustling of many lush trees. She became aware of herself sitting under a tree in the middle of an oasis, watching over the children with a newborn in her arms. Her visions superimposed themselves onto the story of Hajar her mother had told her when she was little. Hajar had despaired for days, alone in the Arabian desert without food or water, a baby in tow until, through Allah's grace, the Zamzam Well sprung with cool, fresh water and saved her and her son's lives. In Mariam's delirium, the woman who was looking after the children shifted from herself to Hajar and back again.

When, against all odds, she was rescued by a Beni-Amer family travelling on the same route across the border to their home in Sudan, and when, seven months later, she gave birth to a son — she hadn't known she was two months pregnant when she'd started her

journey—she remembered her hallucinations and
drew a parallel between her ordeal and Hajar's. Allah
had spared her life and that of the baby she carried, the
way He'd saved Hajar and her son's lives. That's why
she named her boy, her miracle baby, Ismail—after
Hajar's son.

TO AVOID ENGAGING with those around her, Mariam
stared into the distance, past the rows of shoes filling
the hallway from the front door to the kitchen like peb-
bles on a beach. She tried to recall the last time she saw
Ismail opening the front door. She pictured him tilting
his head slightly to the side so he wouldn't hit the door
frame. She remembered how, when he forgot to bend
down and bumped his head, he'd inspect his carefully
groomed, short hair in the hallway mirror, looking for
chips of peeled paint. She focused her attention on the
peephole. From where she sat, it was only a dark spot
on the door. She imagined the impatience on her son's
face as he waited for someone to open the door because
he'd forgotten or lost his keys, which happened often.
She saw the smooth jawline and thin, long neck which,
if it wasn't for peach fuzz on the chin and the prominent
Adam's apple, could have caused him to be mistaken for
a girl. And below that neck, she saw the ghastly, ashen
cut on the jugular again, a distorted, second mouth that
had been sewn shut, as the police had explained, by the

pathologist who'd performed the autopsy. She wished now she hadn't insisted on seeing Ismail's face before the men who performed the *ghusl* at the mosque had tied the cotton shroud over his body in preparation for the *Janazah* prayer and burial. But she needed to see for herself that her miracle baby, the boy who'd survived the trudge from Asmara to Khartoum so early in her pregnancy, the one who, against all odds, had made it through her dehydration and exhaustion, had met his demise in his prime and in this land of peace and plenty. Even now it all felt dubious, as though someone else's image were superimposed over her son's beautiful brown skin. She clenched her teeth remembering the photo shown on the news: a boastful Facebook profile picture that made Ismail look more like a hardened criminal than a murder victim. Why didn't the news people ask her or Ahmed for an appropriate photo? She shook her head and sighed.

She felt an urge to see where her son had drawn his last breath. She wanted to collect his blood from the sidewalk where he was found, wash the ground clean with a soft, wet washcloth as if that pavement were Ismail's body. She didn't want strangers to trample on her son's remains, didn't want her son's blood to dry and settle into the cracks, to become a forgotten, anonymous dust on the thoroughfare of the affluent and indifferent. She owed him at least that, she who had pushed him to his death.

She looked at the two women sitting across from her whispering to each other. These people wouldn't allow her to leave the house. She checked her watch again and sighed. She needed her eldest child by her side. That's all that mattered to her now. Mona was the only one who knew what was in her heart. The guilt and pain that can't be voiced.

"They can't even wash their dead for burial anymore. The risk of contamination is too great," Asma said to the whispering women.

"Can you imagine saying goodbye to your children, to your parents under such circumstances?" one of the women replied, raising her voice and shaking her head.

"If they cared about Black people, I'm sure Ebola would've been history by now," Hayat, Mona's friend, chimed in as she set up the coffee service against the wall in front of the older women.

Mariam dwelled on this concept of Blackness. When she was a little girl, she'd learned from her parents to identify with her tribe, her father's family line especially. She was Saho. She prided herself in knowing her forefathers' names up to seven generations. She knew whom they'd married, how many children they'd each had. As a teenager, she and her family had moved to the capital, Asmara, to help run her father's clothing store. There she'd acquired a new identity: she became Eritrean, finding affinity with people she'd only heard about in her uncles' travel stories, far away from her village, such as the Kunama, Bilen, and Tigre. The war against Ethiopia and the *tegadelti* — rebel fighters — who passionately advocated for the unification of the diverse peoples of the region had reinforced this identity. When she came to Canada, she became African. But *Black* seemed to imply that she was the same as Black Americans and Jamaicans and other Caribbeans with whom she had nothing in common except skin colour.

Mariam was never one of those curious women who revelled in the scraps of information they gathered from the TV news or from what they overheard their husbands discuss. But as Mona and Ismail grew older, they brought home more and more of the outside world. With time, so much of what her children talked about became unintelligible to her, as if the world had expanded while she was busy raising them, often holding down two jobs, or her mind had shrunk as her children grew taller.

As Ismail began to mimic the Black American men on TV, repeating when he thought she wasn't listening the words the rappers spewed, she started to worry about her son's future. All the rappers seemed to do was prance around half-naked, grope scantily clad women, or taunt the viewers and each other with guns. Ismail had tried to explain that not all of it was bad, that some artists talked about real issues affecting Black youth.

"Also, dancehall is Jamaican music, Mom, and hip hop is American," Ismail explained.

But to Mariam's ears, it was all angry noise laced in profanities masquerading as music. She didn't understand why the people who owned the TV stations would put these gangsters on twenty-four hours a day. Didn't they know they were poisoning the minds of boys? She felt ill-equipped to protect her children against the dangers of the vast world outside her doorstep. She became wary of *Black* people.

"What are Blacks in America angry about?" she once wondered aloud as a rap music video came on while she flipped through the TV channels. "In a country as rich as America at that, with none of the language and cultural barriers immigrants like us face," she added. This was before the police shootings of Black people in America started to make the news and before she learned about it from her children.

"Centuries of racism, violence, and discrimination. And still ongoing. You people just don't know," Ismail said, shaking his head.

"All I'm saying is that your father and I didn't come all the way here for our children to turn out like those gangsters. Work hard. That's all you need to do to be successful in this country. So stop watching this nonsense and go study," Mariam said.

"We — all non-white immigrants in this country — should be grateful to African Americans," Mona said, looking up from her cellphone. "They fought *and* continue to fight while the rest of us just waltz in and reap the benefits. You think we could just choose which schools to go to, where to live if it wasn't for the Civil Rights movement? And then you have the nerve, the nerve ... I just can't." Then she stomped away.

Mariam had regretted her question. Mona had a way of showing her exasperation, especially since she started university, a way of talking about rights, choice, and freedom like they were a mother's milk, hers to have whenever she pleased, that disconcerted Mariam.

"We live in Canada," she wanted to tell her daughter but didn't. She thought instead of an Ethiopian proverb about daughters teaching their mothers the ways of childbirth. That's what Canada does to parents, she thought: makes grown people feel as if they're their own children's understudies.

"OH, THERE WAS a case in Spain, just a few days ago," one woman said, snapping Mariam back to the conversation in her living room.

"That'll make them pay attention," Hayat said as she roasted coffee grains on a single burner a few feet away.

"Imagine the victims," another woman said as she cut slices of the *himbasha* Asma had baked. "Coming to terms with your imminent death while soaking in your own excretions and knowing that even the dignity of a proper burial will be denied to you."

"May Allah protect us from such tragedies," Asma said, shaking her head.

Mariam wanted to dismiss these women's argument. To tell them how, when you reached that level of despair and pain, nothing mattered anymore. You didn't think about the how of your burial. Only the living worry about protocol, she wanted to tell them, but she knew they couldn't possibly understand. She closed her eyes to relive that moment in the desert years earlier when the prospect of sleep, painless and eternal, had felt as clear and delightful as cool water. Her body cleansed by hot sand, ready to return to its home. It's the nightmares, if you survived, that were unbearable. Her nightmares were always about being buried alive again and again, choking on sand. They invariably happened when she fell asleep on her back. It even happened once while she was awake. She was caught in a snowstorm when her bus broke down on Fallowfield Road and the surrounding expansive farmland had transformed into a constraining white wall.

WHEN HE TURNED fifteen, Ismail started staying out later and later. As she walked home from the bus stop, after her evening shift, she'd find him standing on a street corner with boys his age, all talking nonsense over each other or just sitting quietly and surveying passersby, acting like the neighbourhood's gatekeepers. Since it was summer, she didn't make much of all this. Besides, he was a boy, what harm could it do? But when she heard that the police frowned upon such gatherings, that they assumed these boys were in gangs or were out selling drugs, she panicked. She'd always expected it would be easier to raise a boy. Back home, daughters were deemed a liability. A mother's negligence to shield her daughter from the violence of men (and failure to curb the trusting inclinations of a girl-child) could ruin the life of a young woman and smear her family's name in shame for generations. But a boy, a first-born son especially, was a family's pride, the one who would provide for and protect his family in lieu of his ageing father. For a mother, a boy was also a piece of herself soaring out and far from the limitations of her lot, her surrogate and even her revenge on the world that confined her. In Canada, it seemed as though the roles were reversed: it was the boys you had to worry about, to keep away from drugs, gangs, the police, and these days from zealots intent on polluting young Muslim minds with violent rhetoric.

Mariam and Ahmed had done their best to teach their children the five tenets of their faith — *shahada, salat, zakat, sawm,* and *hajj* — the way their own parents had done. They encouraged their children to be observant so that their faith could keep them away from the temptations and dangers of the world. But when Mariam learned of young men and women in Europe and even Canada fleeing their families to join fights in the Middle East — she paid close attention to the news now — she was alarmed. For weeks she thought about ways to broach the subject with Ismail before she said: "I hear a Somali youth went to fight in Syria. Do you know him?"

"No," Ismail said as he thumbed his video game controller in the living room. Animated figures of Black men played basketball on the TV screen.

"That's a terrible thing to do to your family," Mariam said.

Ismail shrugged his shoulders.

"I feel for his parents. They left their country because of violence and these stupid boys go looking for wars?"

"It's also really bad what's happening over there, Mom."

"Bad things happen everywhere."

"They're Muslims..."

Mona walked past the living room to the kitchen. "Muslims are killing Muslims," Mona said.

"My son, there are no winners in wars. Muslim or not. That's what they don't tell you. Just countries full of broken people, hollowed-out spirits. I know this from experience." Mariam sat beside her son. "Look at your father," she wanted to add but didn't. Ahmed's childhood trauma was a heavy weight he'd always carried silently, the way she'd kept the details of her own night-mares a secret, even from her husband.

"All those Syrian refugees washing up in Europe —" Ismail said.

Suddenly Mona stood in front of Ismail, blocking his view. "Shut the hell up," she said to him. "Why is no one talking about the Eritrean refugees who have been washing up in Europe for years? You know how many have drowned crossing the Mediterranean Sea? Or the hundreds of thousands of African refugees who have been waiting for asylum for decades in horrible camps? Why don't you show outrage over that?" She was yelling now.

Mariam looked at her daughter with surprise then pride. Usually when Mona got riled up about things, Mariam would just ignore her. Even when Mona wasn't upset, the things she talked about made Mariam feel as though her daughter spoke in riddles just to annoy her. But that day, she recognized her own worry in her daughter's forceful words. She could hear the love. That's what women do, she thought: protect their men from themselves and each other. For the first time, Mariam imagined Mona married and raising her own children, and she felt hopeful.

"Yo, move!" Ismail shouted at his sister. "I don't know nothing about people going to Syria to fight. But as a Muslim . . ."

"But nothing," Mariam said. "Your father and I didn't

sacrifice everything to come here so you kids can have a better future just to see you go and die in someone else's war. You hear me?" She took the controller from his hands. She didn't intend to raise her voice but fear was boiling to the surface and turning into anger.

"Okay, okay, Mom. Jesus. You're always so intense. Relax, I'm not going anywhere. Now can I have that back?" Smiling, he reached for the controller then wrapped his arms around her.

Mariam always found reassurance in Ismail's smile and easy demeanour. No matter how implacable he sometimes appeared to be, she knew she could always reach out to the loving and obedient boy behind the tough facade of his budding manhood. She knew he would not betray her. And through all the troubles he'd faced, no matter how worried she was about his future, deep down, she knew that since Allah had spared them once, He would protect them always. *We've survived worse, you and I*, she would think, holding her son's hand. Whatever the hurdle, things passed eventually, she believed. She often indulged in daydreaming: organizing Mona's and Ismail's weddings, making the *hajj*, welcoming grandchildren and—Allah willing—maybe even great-grandchildren to fill her house with the noise of the big family she always dreamed of.

SHE KNEW THAT parents with means sent their teenagers to summer camps, or enrolled them in music
classes or martial arts. She couldn't afford these things,
so last summer she took Ismail to her cleaning job in
the tall buildings in downtown Ottawa. Ismail re-
luctantly followed her around, picking up trash cans
and dumping the contents in the big bin she wheeled
around from office to office. She spared him the cleaning of the washrooms. As they walked from cubicle to
cubicle, she'd introduce him to some of the younger
lawyers, the chatty ones.

"This could be you someday," she'd tell him, pointing at these young men with their sharp suits, shiny
shoes, and expensive watches.

Ismail would be courteous but abrupt, or unchar-
acteristically sullen, as though he had too much on his
mind to partake in her chatter. Sometimes, he'd quickly
acquiesce, then lean toward her and mutter: "Mom, you
don't have to do that. These people don't care that I'm
your son. Or that you have a family." It was as if he saw
things in the way these young men greeted them, heard
more in their brief exchange than she could fathom.

"Don't be proud, my son," she'd tell him later. "Those
are the kind of friends you should seek. Not those drop-
outs and gangsters you run around with. You have to
choose your friends carefully."

"Those are the guys I grew up with you're talking
about. You know them."

"I don't care. They're in gangs, selling drugs."

"You want me to go across town to make friends. Have you considered the fact that maybe these people wouldn't want to be friends with me?"

He'd pick up the pace as they exited the building.

HAYAT HANDED MARIAM a small cup of hot black coffee. The ginger in the brew left a delicious sting on the tip of Mariam's tongue. One of the other women presented her with a tray of *himbasha*. Mariam shook her head. She took a few more sips and got up to use the bathroom.

Before she opened the bathroom door in the hallway, she looked at the rows of shoes on the floor, almost hoping to find Ismail's sneakers among those of his friends, the boys now gathered in the basement around her husband. Boys barely out of childhood, mastering the difficult work of self-control in the face of loss.

"Are you going to use the bathroom?" Ahmed asked.

She had not seen her husband approach. She became stiff when their eyes met. She grunted then quickly opened the bathroom door. Their two decades of marriage had crumbled in an instant when the police announced Ismail's death. All that was left, the anger, pain, and disappointments, was now laid out between them like a field of broken glass. She sat on the toilet and closed her eyes. She wondered if all the little choices she'd made, all the steps she'd taken in life that didn't mean anything at the time, were all to lead her to this.

Sometimes when she looked at Ahmed, she wondered why she'd followed him into exile. Her father had made a fortune in the textile industry. She could have managed one of his stores on her own. Maybe with time, she would have met a divorcee or a widower she could have married. And yet, she'd left that comfortable life and followed a broken man. A man still struggling not only with the scars of war of his teenage years but also with the shame of having abandoned her in the desert so many years earlier. She had used this guilt against him whenever he'd threatened to kick Ismail out for having dropped out of school or for not seeking employment. The last time this happened, it was a few weeks after one of Ismail's friends was killed outside a nightclub and Ismail had come home so drunk he couldn't stand without leaning on something.

"I can't have you shaming us like this! Get out!" Ahmed had shouted, making a sweeping motion toward the front door with his index finger before he caught Mariam's defiant eyes. Mariam could not bear the idea of her son out in the streets or begging his friends for shelter. It amounted to abandonment.

"You let this boy get away with everything. You're ruining his life," Ahmed had said to her with a tired voice before he went back to bed.

Had she ruined Ismail's life? Would kicking him out have taught him a lesson? There were so many things she'd hidden from her husband to protect Ismail. The fake gun she'd found under her son's mattress. The bag of drugs that she'd thought were herbs until Mona told her otherwise. So many mistakes had marked her path. There were so many things she should have done differently. Coming to terms with who her children were becoming, letting go of her plans, aspirations, and expectation of them was one thing. But this loss, Ismail's death, was a complete annihilation of her reality. What was she if not a mother? And how was she supposed to make up to Ismail for what she had done now that he was gone? Should she go to the police? Would telling the police who she thought was responsible for her son's death amount to snitching? Would that bring about another retaliation against her family?

"Ratting is like digging your own grave," Ismail had told her once while they were watching a crime show on TV.

But like a lot of other things Ismail talked about, this didn't make sense to her then. How was she supposed to know that pressuring her son to do the right thing would cost him his life? Could *she* trust the police? Ismail certainly hadn't. And if she didn't, what was she supposed to do with all this pain? How was she supposed to carry it?

She slid open the small, grilled window for some fresh air. The smell of wood burning nearby took her, as it always did, back in time to her parents' courtyard in Asmara where the soil in her mother's little garden was as red and black as henna on a young bride's feet. She remembered the coal her Quranic teacher ground in a short mortar to make ink and the pieces of wood he sharpened for his students to use to write verses on wood planks they then inscribed to memory. Some sheikhs would wash the words off these boards into a cup and offer the liquid as an elixir to soothe all kinds of ailments. She remembered how Ismail had laughed when she related this and other stories of her childhood to him. How she'd hear him repeat her words to his friends later.

"Yo, mon, that's straight up the craziest shit I've ever heard," his friends would say, their fists like a microphone on their mouths, their fledgling, manly voices reverberating throughout the house.

When a few of his friends stayed over for the night, she'd wake up early in the morning to scramble a dozen eggs and fry two cans of beans with onions, garlic, tomatoes, and peppers to feed their growing bodies. They'd all look so peaceful and young, their bodies spread out on sheets on the living room rug, or on the couches, their lanky legs dangling. And as they walked out of the house as a group after breakfast, she'd wished they were all still small. Maybe if she had not fed Ismail so well, he would have grown up slower and would have stayed safer longer.

The doorbell rang. Mariam felt a bang of pain in her chest. She checked her watch. She waited for a sound, anticipating, hoping it would be Mona. She steadied her grip on the bathroom doorknob before she turned it. She looked out and saw one of Ismail's friends sitting on the steps to the basement, his wide frame stooped, his eyes staring blankly at the wall in front of him. She had seen this kind of gaze on Ismail's face before. The look of surrender in these boys' eyes, when you caught them unguarded, was the kind of defeat she didn't think one could experience outside of a war zone. At least, where she grew up, people clearly knew they were at war. Battles were announced and fought in the open — unlike the vicious violence taking place in dark corners of this city's streets. How many friends had this boy lost? She wondered if those young lawyers in the tall office buildings she cleaned had ever known this kind of loss, this kind of resignation.

When she met Mona's gaze, she saw reflected in her daughter's eyes her own agony, and the tears she had yet to shed. She hesitated for a second before she leaped toward her daughter. Mona's embrace fractured her resistance. She felt a dam breaking. Mother and daughter fell to the ground. Mariam heard a woman rushing toward her and pulling her by the arm.

Asma intervened. "Let her be. She needs to do this," she said.

As she let herself drown in her grief, Mariam felt grateful to Asma.

A howl escaped her throat finally, and then the tears came.

She cried for having betrayed her son the day the police came to question him about a murder in the neighbourhood. The threat and urgency in the police officers' voices had frightened her to the core, so without thinking, she'd ran to the utility room where she knew Ismail had hidden a big sharp knife with a scalloped handle. She'd seen a boy hand it to him the night before. She didn't want her son to get in trouble for someone else's crime. But after handing the knife to the cops, when she'd turned to explain to Ismail why this needed to be done, the hate and anger in his eyes, the clenched jaws and fists, had instantaneously transformed her son into someone she'd never seen before.

She cried for having pushed him again a few days later, at the detention centre on Innes Road. When she advised him through the glass partition to cooperate with the cops, to tell them whatever he knew to save his life, Ismail had refused.

"You don't understand, Mom, I can't," he'd whispered, surveying his surroundings from the corners of his eyes.

Mariam had examined the police officers stationed at each end of the room. Then she'd turned to the young inmates sitting on either side of Ismail, talking to their own families. Their uniforms, closed faces and fists, their defiant air; they resembled her son and she hated them for it. She had to do whatever it took to get him out of there. That's why she'd resorted to begging and crying noisily, relating for the first time how she'd risked her life to come to Canada.

"I wish I had died back then so I could have been spared this day," she wailed.

When she looked up, Ismail's eyes had turned red, as though he'd just cried too. Even though he'd stayed stoic and distant for the remainder of the visitation, she knew his resolve had softened. She felt victorious, capable, in control.

"I LOVE YOU, MOM," Mona said through her own cries, and hugged Mariam harder.

For a long time, Mariam had resisted saying *I love you* back to her children. It felt ridiculous to her, this stating of the obvious. Love to her was in how you woke up before your children and got their things ready for school, how you stayed up late even after a twelve-hour shift to make them tea when they studied for exams. Love was in how you pressed their clothes, combed their hair; in the way you disciplined them, trying to instill values you inherited from your own parents; in how you held their hands before they left you to go study in another city across the country the way Mona had done; in the many complicated dishes you prepared for days for when they finally came home; and in how you watched them eat as if they hadn't eaten in days because they missed your cooking. But today, Mona's words felt like a healing balm on a throbbing cut. They made Mariam miss hearing those words from Ismail's mouth. He used to say them so often, she realized now, she had long stopped hearing them.

ON THE DAY of Ismail's testimony, Ahmed, Mona, and Mariam had taken a seat on the benches behind Ismail's lawyer in clear view of the witness box. Mariam had looked at two thick folders in the lawyer's hands, wondering why her son's short life needed so many pages, so many words to defend his innocence. She'd felt her heart shatter when she saw Ismail come through a side door escorted by an officer, his hands and feet in shackles. And when her son looked at her as he took a seat in the witness box, she knew something had irrevocably changed in him. Though she didn't understand most of what was said that day, though it took his death for her to finally grasp the retaliatory laws of the streets Ismail had to abide by, she'd understood the message in Ismail's gaze when he looked at her before pointing at the accused in the glass box against the wall: *You made me do this.*

heading somewhere

OMAR TYPES *DOMESTIC WORKERS SYRIA* AND waits for the page to load. Images swirl in his mind like a gutted photo album set to the wind: his old girlfriend Sara, his childhood friends Meseret and Naima, another girl or two whose names he can't remember. Young women who'd left Addis Ababa to work as maids in Saudi Arabia, Syria, and elsewhere, light on luggage and high on anticipation for a better life. Words chase these images like guided missiles — *isolation, beating, rape,* and *murder* (disguised as *suicide*) — but Omar doesn't want to think about these things right now. He wills his mind in another direction: Sara wading through Damascus's narrow, winding streets, past busy, dusty souks — a landscape he only knows from pictures he'd googled recently — to find a way out of Syria before civil war engulfs the city.

It's only 4:15 p.m. but the snow cloaking the quiet Ottawa neighbourhood is already turning to soft indigo. Omar hopes to find a lead into Sara's whereabouts or at least a contact number before his wife, Marianne, comes home from work in an hour.

The rebels have taken control of Douma, a city only ten kilometers away from Damascus, he'd heard announced on the news last night.

Sara might already be in one of the NGOs' makeshift shelters, waiting for a flight home. If only Ethiopia had an embassy in Syria ... or maybe she's on her way to the Ethiopian consulate in Beirut. He keeps speculating, as he's been doing for the last two days, ever since Sara's mother called from Addis Ababa to ask him for help in getting her daughter out of Damascus.

When he was little, back in Addis Ababa, whenever he and his friends heard screams coming from the police station adjacent to their compound, they'd rush to stack up boxes, tires, or any piece of trash solid enough to stand on against the concrete wall separating the compound from the station so they could glimpse whomever was being interrogated that day. Sara would already be there beside him, her eyes sparkling eagerly. Together, they'd dare other children to join them. Serious interrogations were done behind closed doors so only screams and echoes of unintelligible words could be heard, but the kids would line up beside each other anyway, stand on tiptoe and crane their little heads over the wall, hoping to see some poor, petty criminal writhe and scream on the dusty court surrounded by police officers beating on him with batons and straps. Sometimes, an officer would catch them watching and threaten to lock them up, wagging a finger and cursing, or even flinging rocks at them. They'd all run away, clumsily tripping over their cobbled-together stands, down dirt paths riddled with potholes and sharp rocks half-buried in the soil, to their homes. Some would be on the verge of tears by the time they stopped, but not Sara. She would laugh, her mischievous eyes wild with exhilaration. Omar loved and hated that about her. He admired her fearlessness and yet lived in constant worry that in the eyes of their peers, she, a girl, might one day prove to be the braver of the two.

This childhood memory melts into a sadness in Omar's gut. He shakes his melancholy away, opens a link, and scans through the news:

We heard gunfire and we saw black smoke behind the buildings but our employer told us there was a celebration at the army barracks.

We wanted to return home but our employers left the country and we were locked inside their house.

Stranded migrant workers should contact their embassies or the International Organization for Migration (IOM) for repatriation assistance...

He spots a link to the IOM and learns they have an office in Damascus. He frantically clicks and clicks again until he finds their contact information. On a piece of paper he writes down the IOM's number, under the one Sara's mother had given him to reach her daughter at her employers' house. He adds the Ethiopian Consulate's number in Beirut to the list. He opens another link or two, then gives up. The news is too depressing to continue reading. He tucks the piece of paper in his shirt pocket. He'll call early tomorrow morning. It'll be afternoon in that part of the world by then. He'll also try Sara's employers' house again. He closes his laptop, picks up his winter coat from the hallway closet, closes the front door behind him, and heads to the grocery store a few blocks away.

HOLDING THE CORNER post for balance, Sara climbs onto the patio chair. She wraps the bedsheet she's tied to the ledge like a rope around her arm and slowly climbs over her employers' second-floor balcony and down to the quiet street below. Unlike her Filipina neighbour who ran to her government's embassy in the city, Sara had to find a way out of Damascus and into Beirut where she could seek help from the Ethiopian consulate. A metre or so before her feet touch the ground, she loses her grip and falls on the asphalt. She gets up quickly, adjusts the duffle bag on her back, and looks up toward the house. The lights have not been turned on. She takes a deep breath and searches the dark street for the ride Mohamed, her employers' gatekeeper, had arranged for her. She spots an old van a few metres away. Its brake lights flash twice, as agreed upon. She walks toward it as fast as she can without running.

"Get in the back," the driver says from the half-open window before Sara has a chance to make eye contact.

"Cover yourself with that blanket and keep your head down," he orders with a rushed voice.

Panic takes over as she slides the van door shut. What if this is a trap? She trusts Mohamed. He didn't usually let her out of the compound alone for fear of losing his job but he was nice to her. And he has delivered on the promise of finding her someone who, for a fee, would help her. But this man could be taking her to the police station instead of the outskirts of Damascus where she's supposed to meet another man who will take her to Beirut. She shakes the distressing thought away. There is nothing she can do now but hope for the best.

She squeezes her slim body between two rows of seats as an extra precaution. Mohamed had said the military was intensifying its operations in the city and that soldiers have been stopping and searching cars often these days. She rests her head on her duffle bag and covers herself with the blanket. The man starts the car and heads toward Jawaher Lal Nahro.

For a while, she listens through the van's rattles for any changes in speed or signs of abnormal noise outside. Then, to ease her anxiety, she tries to think of happier times. Her earliest memory is of Ababa Tesfaye's children's TV show. Every Saturday at 6 p.m., she, Omar, and other neighbourhood kids would gather at the entrance of Emama Elsabet's living-room-turned-bar. Wriggling around each other to get to the front of the line, they'd watch Emama Elsabet as she heaved herself onto a short wooden stool, removed the crocheted doily from the small TV on the shelf in the corner above the glass bar, and turned the dial to on. The children would then rush to get the best spot by the side door, from where they could watch their favourite show without disturbing Emama Elsabet's customers. Some nights, there would be too many kids to fit in the tight space assigned to them. Fighting would erupt and the bar owner would shoo everybody home, cursing. On good days, though, they'd sit there, all senses glued to that TV, like seedlings turned to the sun, lost in Ababa Tesfaye's tales of smart foxes and gullible little children, of greedy humans and misunderstood snakes. They'd sit on the chilly red-and-black-checkered cement tiles for an hour, their scrawny little bodies huddled together for warmth against the cold air coming through the open door. They'd return Ababa Tesfaye's greetings, answer his questions, and cheer in unison when Good prevailed against Evil. Once in a while, Emama Elsabet or one of her waitresses would instruct them to keep quiet.

Back then, Omar wanted to follow in Ababa Tesfaye's footsteps, and Sara dreamed of becoming an actress or a singer, anything to get her on TV. Together, they would memorize Ababa Tesfaye's stories and re-enact them in front of their friends and families. How strange and remote that part of her life feels now, as though she's lived two consecutive lives connected only by brittle threads of memory.

SARA LOOKS AROUND hoping to find a familiar face. A dozen African and Asian men and women are sitting on the shabby linoleum floor, all staring at the dirty walls in front of them or at their own hands. None of them is *Habesha*. A piece of fabric that might once have served as a tablecloth curtains the only window in the room. A light bulb hanging low from the ceiling bathes the room with a dim orange hue. This apartment must be in one of Damascus's western suburbs, near the border into Lebanon. That's what Mohamed had told her, but her driver had only grunted when she asked him to confirm this as he dropped her off. She sits beside a Black woman with a dirty shawl around her shoulders and waits for the car that will clandestinely transport them into Lebanon.

"Where are you from?" Sara asks her neighbour.

A tuft of hair has escaped from the woman's several-months-old braids as if someone had pulled her by the hair.

"Uganda," the woman replies without turning, her voice cracking a little.

Sara waits for a second. "I'm from Ethiopia," she volunteers.

The woman nods slightly without looking at her.

Sara leaves the woman to her silence, folds her legs closer to her chest, and discreetly takes out a piece of paper from her bra. She examines the portrait-size picture of Jesus in her palm, one of the few things the recruiters at the employment agency had not confiscated when she came to work in Damascus ten months ago. If only they hadn't taken her cellphone or the thin gold necklace Omar had given her before he left for Canada. She could have sold them and used the money now.

"You know, your saviour seems more in need of saving than the people he presides over," Omar had said once, pointing with his chin at a framed portrait of Jesus her mother hung on the wall above the credenza in their living room. Making fun of each other's religion was a subtle way they had of testing the parameters of a possible future together.

"I prefer him to your faceless Allah," she'd retorted.

Now, staring at Jesus's soft golden hair flowing like mead around His oval, blemish-free face, His big childish blue eyes, His delicate hand pointing at a heart that resembles the strawberries her madam reserved for important guests, Sara wonders if her innocent and fragile-looking God could indeed save her from the nightmare she's in. She quickly shakes the blasphemous thought away, cautiously crosses herself, and tucks the picture back into her bra.

OMAR PICKS UP a plastic basket from a pile by the grocery store's entrance and joins a crowd of after-work shoppers. He chooses a pack of whole-wheat spaghetti from the pasta and sauce aisle and heads to the organic produce section. He squeezes through a mostly white and middle-class group of people who are, with the seriousness of a physician examining patients, stroking ripe mangoes and pears or studying the crispiness of leafy vegetables. He grabs a bag of mixed greens and walks past other patrons comparing the nutritional values of condiments in tiny jars and takes his place at the end of the express lane.

He prefers regular pasta but Marianne is big on healthy eating except for her weekly indulgence of a Big Mac, poutine, and Diet Coke. He once or twice pointed out the irony of the Diet Coke in this meal, but to no avail. His wife can be stubborn sometimes, not very unlike Sara, except Marianne's unyielding nature comes from a life of comfort, free of wants and doubts.

He admires Marianne's assurance, her deep-seated confidence that nothing is out of reach, that every broken thing or person is potentially repairable. That must be what she saw in him, his potential; he was someone she could save and fix.

It was pure chance, how he'd met Marianne. She, a Canadian foreign service officer on her first mission abroad, had accompanied the new Canadian consular officer to a function organized by the Ethiopian Tourism Commission to welcome new foreign diplomats; he, a third-year Addis Ababa University student, had escorted a distant aunt, a bureaucrat at the Ministry of Culture and Tourism, to the event in lieu of her ailing husband. Marianne would tell him later how she'd watched him from afar as he talked his way around the room, mesmerized by the ease with which he carried himself despite his apparent youth and the ill-fitting blazer he wore. And how a rush of curiosity and desire had taken her over, a wonderful stirring of the heart she hadn't felt in the year and a half she'd lived in Addis Ababa. And how, surprising even herself, she'd accepted his offer to show her around the city — even though she'd already seen all the tourist spots — to satisfy a sudden need to be wooed by a tall, handsome man.

The day he left Addis Ababa a married man, he'd stood outside the bedroom he'd shared with his three brothers, his eyes travelling from one corner of the room to the next, trying to look at his childhood's landscape from the perspective of his future Canadian self, as he imagined a cartographer or an archeologist would do upon discovering an ancient site. Would he recognize the way the sun's rays, nonchalant as only eternal things can afford to be, spread on his single bed, diluting the brown sheets to a soft caramel tone? Would he recognize the sandalwood smell that clung to every corner of the two-room house from his mother's daily incense burning to voracious spirits who'd never answer her prayers? Would he remember the names of the girls whose initials he and his brothers carved on the legs of their wooden beds when they were teenagers? He didn't want to forget these things. Others, he wished to erase: the ugliness of the newspaper-covered dirt walls, the paper brown and stiff in places from water damage; the smell of urine in the pink plastic chamber pot his mother kept under her bed for when it was too late to go to the communal bathroom at the other end of the compound; the misery and hunger that forced him and his siblings to work as shoe-shiners and street vendors before they were ten years old.

Rivulets of cold sweat had run down his armpits as he walked past rows of old, pastel-coloured houses and their rundown verandas on his way to the car that would take him to the airport. He'd felt a little dazed, like a prisoner stuck on the threshold between dream and reality, his mother's hold on his arm as she limped beside him the only weight constantly grounding him back into the tangible world.

On their way out of the compound, he'd stopped in front of the little house Sara shared with her parents. He'd stared at what must have once been deep bright red steps where Sara and other neighbourhood girls used to play marbles when they were little, now turned to the colour of raw beet skin. It was on these steps that he'd said goodbye to her the night before, and where he'd promised to send her sponsorship papers as soon as he could. He'd wished he had the power to fuse her body onto his then, melt flesh on flesh and mind to heart, so he could take something real of her with him, so he could reassure her of his love and commitment, convince her that Marianne meant nothing to him, was only a means to an end, a gateway to their future happiness in Canada. But he was never good at serious talk. His was the language of a street hustler and Sara knew all his tricks.

THE WOMAN IN front of Omar in the grocery store's express lane leans her head to the side of the line then turns to him and says: "It's never going to stop, is it?" And to Omar's perplexed look, she adds, "The snow," pointing at a wall of white outside the store's sliding doors.

Omar nods.

"I wish I was in Jamaica right now. Or anywhere else but here."

"Be careful of what you wish for," Omar says with a sly smile.

The woman looks at him, puzzled for a moment. Then she says, "Well, not anywhere, but you know what I mean. Some place warm and pleasant."

Omar nods again and scrolls through his cellphone, looking for missed unknown or international calls.

The Canadian embassy has already closed its office in Damascus. Otherwise, he would have asked Marianne to contact one of her colleagues there to help him find Sara. His wife has always been a little touchy about his history with Sara, but this is too important. Marianne would have put her feelings aside, at least until Sara was out of harm's way. The tension, innuendos, and outright accusations might have started again later, the way they did last year when Omar, too busy planning his first trip back to Ethiopia, and too absorbed by the prospect of seeing Sara again, had neglected Marianne. Thankfully, his wife didn't go as far as threatening him with a divorce as he had feared. He resented Marianne her power—divorce meant the loss of his permanent resident card, maybe even deportation. More importantly, though, he was furious with himself for having let his guard down with her. However, things are different now between Sara and him, and his wife probably knows that.

LAST YEAR, after four years in Canada, Omar had finally made it to Addis Ababa for a month-long visit. And Sara had just returned home from a three-year stint in Dubai. At first, their reunion was all that Omar had hoped it would be. The outburst of contagious joy that was her laughter had become somehow dimmer, her manners more poised. Still, her face had retained the fullness of her teenage years and under the restrained demeanour she wore like a protective veil, he could discern the contours of the vivacious girl he grew up with. But it didn't take long before his excitement was shattered. In tightly knit communities like theirs, secrets rarely stay hidden. His best friend, Alemayehu, was the first to tell him what Sara had been up to in Dubai.

When he confronted her, to his surprise, she didn't deny the allegations nor did she try to repent.

"I did what I had to do...just as you did," she said.

He could taste the venom in her contained voice, the sarcasm in her dry laughter afterwards. He felt a gush of hatred toward her for implying that marrying Marianne for Canadian citizenship was akin to the life of prostitution she'd chosen. Why didn't she just return home after she'd run away from her abusive employers' house? He wished he could lay his hands on the nameless people that had pushed her into such degradation.

"I couldn't come home empty-handed," she'd said. "I went there to make money."

He should have known that Sara couldn't have allowed herself to give up on her responsibilities. If a lifetime of struggle teaches anything to someone as strong willed as Sara, it's perseverance.

What surprised him most later on was that their last confrontation was not infused with insults and tears the way their fights used to be; their final breakup was not inscribed in a specific, single instance that he could replay in his mind. Instead, the irreparability of the matter was felt rather than heard, the reality of it taken in slowly, like the smell of rot carried by a light breeze over a distance. Only recently did he realize why his anger had, for so long, felt muddied, unripe for outburst, his vexation rigged with confusion and despair: it hid his own shame. The shame of a man who'd failed to protect the woman he loved.

If only everyone he trusted had not joined the others in vilifying Sara. "City girls can't handle hard work. You'd never hear of village girls debasing themselves that way," said his old neighbour, a woman who'd known both Sara and him since they were babies.

"A Muslim girl would not have done that," his mother said.

But he can't blame anyone. No matter how modern he believed himself to be, he just couldn't shed the image of other men possessing Sara's warm, lithe body. It had damaged the truth of his love for her and sullied the dream he had for them.

For months after returning to Canada, he'd felt as though he was afflicted with permanent jet lag. Even the childhood memories he used to cherish turned to ashes in his mind. For a while, the only thing he clearly remembered about his trip was the clinking sound of the gold bracelets Sara wore daily as if to remind herself it was all worth it.

Now, surrounded by people who have never experienced the stink of abject poverty, a new truth reveals itself to him: Sara might pay for his ego with her life, caught in the crossfire of a civil war. Would he be able to live with himself if something happened to her in Syria? Why did she have to go to Syria anyway, as though Dubai was not bad enough?

The woman in front of him in the express lane interrupts his thoughts again. "I bet it's always warm where you're from."

"Yes," Omar says and turns his head left and right, pretending to be searching for someone.

On any other day, he would have been more receptive. He would have told the woman about Addis Ababa's two-thousand-kilometre-high altitude, the blazing sun in January and the cold teeth-shattering early morning wind at the height of the rainy season in July. He would have told her about the hail, sometimes as big as ping-pong balls, that crackled against his house's tin roof like popcorn. He would have told her how, when he was little, sometimes he'd collect hail from his neighbours' front yards in his mother's rusted enamel bucket then dump it in front of his house, spread it around quickly before it melted, and pretend he lived in America, which in his mind at that time encompassed the whole of Europe and Canada. But not today. Today, he just wants to get to the cash register, pay for his groceries, and go home. He wants the churning in his stomach to stop. He wants the night to end so he can try to contact Sara tomorrow.

SARA BRUSHES HER arm against her small chest to feel the thin wad of cash in her bra. There's just enough money to cover the fare to Beirut and some food. She's going home empty-handed. She bites her lower lip hard to stifle the anger in her throat, then remembers her surroundings: she might not make it out of Syria at all. She realizes that she shouldn't have come to Damascus, but how could a poor girl with only a high school diploma and average looks achieve anything in a country of tens of millions of unemployed youth?

She imagines her mother counting and recounting what's left of the money she'd sent her four months earlier, devising ways to make it last until the next time. But there won't be a next time. The money Sara made in Dubai was supposed to have been enough to supplement her father's modest income. She had dreamed of her parents running a small business together, perhaps a pastry shop, working side by side, filled with a joy only a sense of recovered dignity and pride can bring. She had even fancied she'd have enough extra money to cover her flight to Canada when Omar sent her the sponsorship papers he'd promised. Instead, all that money and all the gold Abu Karim — the old Emirati widower whose mistress she'd been for a year before his sons kicked her out of his house — was spent on her father's medical bills when his diabetes suddenly attacked his vision and kidneys.

"My ma'am was killed when she was coming home from her friend's house. A bomb fell on the building next door and took her life," Sara hears a middle-aged woman sitting across from her say to her neighbour. "Everybody was running and crying. I went to my ma'am's room and took money from where she hides it and ran away."

"The taxi driver I paid to bring me here almost handed me over to the police," a young man said to the middle-aged woman. "I open the car door and run away when I saw the police station sign."

"My ma'am refused to give me food. She beat me until I was unconscious. I was not sorry she died," the middle-aged woman said, adjusting her shawl on her head.

Sara looks down at her sweat-stained clothes, her jeans dirty from when she fell as she jumped out of her employers' house, her fingernails chipped and dirty. How self-conscious she'd felt last year when she first saw Omar in Addis Ababa after four years. He had greeted her with open arms and the same boyish smile she remembered. He'd hugged her, too, but his embrace was tentative, as if he were suddenly unable to trust the memory of their intimacy. Although she didn't recognize his scent, she hoped he'd recall the perfume she wore, the one he'd bought her long before he'd left for Canada.

She sat across from him in one of the two wooden chairs in his mother's living room. In the dim light, she searched his face for signs of time's passage or the strains of distance that might have altered her knowledge of him. Omar's dark skin, which used to glow like freshly roasted coffee beans in the summer, had gotten lighter, his body fleshy, yet not fat. She thought it suited him, but these manifestations of comfort had proved her fear right: time and circumstances had erected an insurmountable barrier between them.

She'd tucked her dry hands between her thighs, rubbing them together in the folds of her skirt to smooth out their coarseness and, by the same token, the memories of the years spent in Dubai, first cooking, scrubbing floors, and washing eight people's clothes by hand. And then, after her employer made it a habit of forcing himself on her whenever his wife and children were away, of sleeping with men for pay.

"If you can't stop them, might as well have them pay for it," a girlfriend had said to her.

She had found it hard at first, but like anything else in life, only the first steps were unbearable. She was lucky to have attracted Abu Karim's eye. Within a month, she had gone from a battered maid to a prostitute to a live-in mistress. But some scars are hard to conceal. Omar's gaze was a burning sun melting her cover. If he ever saw her naked again, she was sure he'd be able to discern the outlines of Abu Karim's pale, spotty hands as the old man squeezed her thighs until they hurt in a pathetic attempt to summon his long-lost vigour, and the foul lust of all the others before him.

Only the state of Omar's mother's house quieted her fears a little. Nothing in the living room had been moved or replaced in decades. His mother's single bed with its thin mattress occupied one dark wall. Another corner housed the family's modest belongings, piled up under an old bedsheet. She was abashed by the fact that noticing these things improved her mood, made her think that perhaps Omar was not as out of reach as she had thought.

"How was Dubai?" he'd asked, with his usual playful tone, as if she'd only been away on a short vacation, with the same honeyed voice that sometimes made it hard for her to take him seriously. "I'm so relieved you're back for good," he'd added before she had time to respond, turning her irritation into a yearning in her throat—he had not yet heard about what had happened in Dubai.

Her eyes followed the fat vein above his left eyebrow, the only sign she knew of his nervousness. It travelled up in an uncertain path and forked right under his hairline, dividing his forehead into two, almost identical, flat planes. She ached to follow its path with her finger the way she used to. She wanted to tell him how, when she first moved to Dubai, often, when she found her employers' prayer rugs laid out on the floor, she'd think of him. When the whole family went out shopping or to visit with friends, she'd lie down on the floor beside the rug and, propped on her elbow, brush her palm against the velvety prints of minarets and the Kaaba, follow the intricate patterns of arabesque and mysterious words embroidered into the fabric, all the while dreaming of his fingers on her skin.

"Take your dirty hands off my prayer rug, *ya kafira!*" her madam had yelled at her once, bursting into the room and swinging her shopping bags at her. Sara knew not to touch the Quran but didn't know a rug could also be too precious for her Christian hands. Nevertheless, she'd felt such a perverse pleasure seeing her madam's reaction that she wished she could tell her about the sexual thoughts she'd just had. Later on, lying on her thin mattress on the kitchen floor where she slept, she'd wondered if Omar would have disapproved too.

Jealousy and competition are rife among those who manage to find work in the Middle East, so it was only a matter of time before her secret was out. She tried to tell Omar of the abuse that led her to prostitution. She wanted him to know that every time her employer attacked her, she fought him off with all her might, and that, when he invariably overpowered her, she refused to look at his face, keeping her eyes shut or on the ceiling to deny him the acknowledgement he sought. But she couldn't find words to describe her ordeal.

Once Omar found out what had happened, he couldn't look her in the eye or touch her, as though she had become a leper overnight. At least in the eyes of the other neighbours, she could see envy mixed with disapproval as they ogled her foreign-made clothes and gold jewellery. His attitude enraged her. She snickered at his discomfort, donning the protective mask of an only girl-child who'd learned at an early age that laughter can be as powerful an arsenal against fear or shame as a fist. What did he expect her to do? Run back home and wait for him to rescue her? Yet, after the heat of the moment had passed, she wished Omar would see through her facade and that, once the shock of the news had subsided from his mind, he'd come back to her.

She should have known better. No matter how much things have changed from the time of her parents, women will always bear the brunt of any transgression. "The markings of Eve's daughters," her mother would have said. Why did she expect Omar to be above this?

She only admitted her defeat after he'd left for Canada again, this time with just a vague promise to keep in touch. How naive she'd been for thinking that they could someday pick up from where they'd left off four years earlier when, for months, she'd lived spellbound by Omar's vivid aspirations for their future together. The way he held her close that night on her parents' doorstep, dragging out the moment of separation before he'd left. In spite of herself, she'd believed in his power to whisk her away from that miserable neighbourhood, that dead-end of a life.

"Good riddance. What did you expect from a Muslim?" her mother had said in an attempt at consolation, but both women knew that what Sara had done would always cling to her, staining her chances of marriage to any man, Muslim or Christian. Her only choice was to go back to the Middle East, make good money, and support her family, not wallow in self-pity.

OMAR TAKES THE spaghetti sauce he and Marianne had prepared on the weekend out of the freezer and places it in the microwave. He leans on the granite countertop and watches the day die outside his window, the suburban desolation turn into a dim crescent moon of serenity. He opens the box of whole-wheat spaghetti he bought and adds the contents to the hot water on the stove. With his palm, he slowly pushes the tips of the dry pasta into the water as the submerged parts soften and curve.

His cellphone rings.

"Hon, can you run and pick up some salad and a dessert? I'm stuck in traffic," his wife says through an ambulance siren in the distance.

"I got the salad but not dessert."

"You know how much my mom loves cake ... Please?"

He had forgotten his in-laws were coming to dinner tonight. Irritation mounts in him. He has always been good at massaging people's egos into liking him, except for his in-laws. In five years, he hasn't been able to get through to them. Whenever they show interest in him, it feels suspect, their insinuations just out of reach of his rugged English. His mother-in-law annoys him: her perfectly coiffed salt-and-pepper hair, stiff and flat on her head, her big inquisitive eyes and non-stop chatter. She makes him think of a grey parrot. She uses words such as "marvellous" or "extraordinary" after every sentence he utters, equally impressed by his ability to remove stains from carpets as she is by his answers to questions about his life back home. His father-in-law's approach is more direct, more directly aimed at emasculating him.

"Trust me, baby, it might come off wrong to you but they don't mean any harm," Marianne would say once they're alone, wrapping her plump arms around his neck. "They're just old and set in their old ways, you know? Anyway, you'll graduate soon, get a good job, and make Daddy proud, okay?" she'd tease, guiding his hands to her ample breasts.

He can't complain, though. Marianne has been good to him. After his trip to Ethiopia, he'd decided to leave his stained past with Sara behind and fully embrace the comfortable and uncomplicated life Marianne offered. "Home is what you make it," he'd heard someone say on the bus once. And this saying had stayed with him. After all, he'd come a long way, so why provoke fate by wanting to have it all? And until now, this thought had sustained him.

The clock above the hickory kitchen cabinets chimes 6 p.m. He turns the stove off and strains the cooked noodles in a colander. He should have just waited until Marianne was home to boil the pasta.

As he picks up his winter coat from the hallway closet again, he catches a glimpse of his reflection in the hallway mirror. His mind leaps toward Sara again. The little girl who laughed off the officers' threats at the police station next to their compound. Her devilish glee. And the other, grown one, who stood up to his condemnation with fortitude and pride. He decides to call Sara one more time before he heads out to the grocery store. He puts his winter coat down on a stool in the kitchen and reaches in his shirt pocket for the piece of paper where he'd written Sara's employers' number and a calling card. He dials the numbers on the calling card first, then Sara's employers'.

"May I speak to Sara, please," he says, surprised that the line connected on the first try this time. "I'm her cousin, calling from Canada," he continues, as Sara's mother had instructed him to do to avoid raising any suspicion.

"From Canada?" the man on the other end asks, his voice full of sleep. "Wait."

Omar hears grumbling in the background. He imagines the man explaining the late-night call to his wife. He pictures Sara apologizing to them as she hurries to the phone. He feels a nervous rush overcome his body. He takes a deep breath and tries to rehearse what he will say to her but the sentences disappear before he's done forming them.

The voices at the other end of the line become louder. He hears a man and a woman arguing but he can't understand what they're saying. After what seems like an hour, the man picks up the phone and with an accusatory tone says: "She's not here. She is gone."

Before Omar has time to ask any more questions, the man yells at him in Arabic and hangs up.

Omar stares at the phone in his hand, trying to understand what just happened. He starts to dial the number again. Then it dawns on him: Sara has managed to escape from her employers' house.

He picks up his winter jacket again, closes the door behind him, and faces the shimmering snow dancing in the wind. What really bothers him is not so much what she'd done but what others had done to her body. This knowledge still digs into his chest like a crooked rib and there isn't much he can do about it. He stands in the doorway for a moment. He focuses on a thought forming in the back of his consciousness, the way a photographer sharpens the contours of an image by manipulating the lens. Maybe it's the fresh cold air that clears his mind a little or maybe it's the small piece of good news he'd just heard, but he feels hope, a small and shrivelled hope that's true, but one that's as flammable as tinder. Perhaps with time, he'll learn to live with that nudging in his chest the way people accept their wounds when they realize they won't die from them. Another hope he nurses is that Sara will forgive him for having broken his promise to sponsor her and for having shunned her for doing what she had to do. This one is the most fragile of his aspirations.

He touches his chest on the side where the piece of paper with Sara's contact numbers is tucked in his shirt pocket as if this gesture might nudge events toward a favourable outcome. He takes a deep breath to alleviate the guilt, worry, and longing inside then walks into the dark night to the same grocery store, thinking of how ludicrous the idea of a grown person demanding dessert after each meal would sound to anyone back home.

SARA'S EMPLOYERS WILL soon notice she's gone. They have treated her fairly; they even took her on a vacation to their village by the sea once, although she would have preferred a few days off instead. Nonetheless, they'd re-fused to give her her passport back when she told them last week she wanted to return home. Instead, they dismissed her worries and tried to appease her, prom-ising that if the rebels pushed any closer to Damascus, they'd take her out of Syria themselves. If she'd learned anything from her time in the Middle East, it was not to trust any Arab. Even her friend Lily, who is lucky enough to work for a nice couple in Kuwait that let her call long distance for free, had agreed with her.

She wonders if Omar is worrying about her at this instant, as she waits in a filthy room for a van that might or might not come. Or if he is leading the life of a Canadian man with his Canadian wife in a safe and comfortable Canadian home, oblivious to the misery or dangers of a world thousands of kilometres away from his. She tries in vain to imagine him at a dinner table with his wife. Her memory of his physique is frozen in a picture he'd sent her a few months after he'd moved to Ottawa: the wide collars of his winter jacket turned up to his ears, his slender body scrunched up, his smile like a grimace of pain. He looked as if he were being swallowed by the whitewashed Canadian landscape of clouds and snow and imploring the viewer to rescue him. She'd felt such anguish for him then. It's his turn now. She wants him to be worried sick for her. She wants him gutted by guilt and remorse. After all, it's his fault she's in this mess.

She stretches her legs in front of her and pulls a water bottle out of her bag. She takes a few sips and passes it to her neighbour, examining the woman as she gulps down the rest. She wonders if this woman is thinking about some man too. And if she's despising herself for thinking of him at a time like this. For caring about what he thought, what he did, if he'd come back to her or wait for her, whatever the case may be.

She gets up and paces back and forth, unconcerned with her travel companions' stares, then stops in her tracks to listen to the muffled voices of men outside the closed door. A man wearing a heavy wool jacket with a few buttons missing opens the door and with the urgency of the hunted yells: "*Yalla*, get up, the car is here!"

The Ugandan woman jerks her head right to left and again but remains seated, as though she has been tricked one too many times to trust her luck now. Sara picks up her duffle bag with one hand and extends an arm to help the woman up. She attempts an encouraging smile even though her own heart is beating so violently she fears it might break out of her chest, taking her life with it. But if she has to die, she would rather die on the move, heading somewhere.

Everyone shuffles through the apartment door. The freezing strong January wind washes over Sara's face, dousing her nervousness. In the distance, a muezzin calls the faithful to prayer. The travellers hand their fare to the man in the wool jacket and one by one take their seats in an old Toyota HiAce that reminds Sara of the minivan taxis that are ubiquitous in Addis Ababa's streets. She takes her seat in the tightly packed, beat-up van for the hour or so ride to Beirut. As the vehicle starts to move, she leans her head against the headrest and covers her nose and mouth with her scarf against the smell of sweat and exhaust fumes.

She thinks of what could happen if they get caught after they cross the border. Would the Lebanese hand them over to the Syrians? She thinks of the possibility of dying here. The thought of leaving this earth without seeing Omar again, without any hope for reconciliation, digs a hole in her heart. She thinks of all the ways people have of hurting each other. She'd practised letting Omar fade from her consciousness, piece by piece. *Eventually I'll just go on living, as people always do*, she'd told herself time and again. Was she wrong to have sneered at his reaction? Was she too selfish, too hard-headed? They have been a part of each other's lives since childhood. All that entangled history, all the memories: some hard and painful like ice, others as warm and nourishing as summer rain. Some of it might eventually dissipate but she knows Omar will endure in her mind and body for a very long time. And if she dies before she makes it home, she knows she will linger in Omar's memories as well. Of this much she is certain. But she can't indulge in regrets and hope for a future with him right now. What's important, what has so far stood the test of time, is her will to fight, her determination to hold herself together. And to make it home, to her parents'. The other home, the one she once dreamed up with Omar, might have after all only been just that: a dream.

Sara feels someone shaking her by the arm. She opens her eyes and looks at the Ugandan woman beside her. The woman points at dim lights in the distance: "Lebanon?" she asks, suddenly realizing it was possible to make it out of Syria.

Sara rubs her eyes to clear her mind of sleep, surprised that she'd dozed off. She checks her watch: it has been forty minutes since they left the apartment in Damascus. At the horizon, the pink dusty sky has started to extract itself from the dark mountains.

"Should be. But I don't know," she says. "Did the driver stop anywhere? A checkpoint?"

The woman gives Sara a puzzled look.

"Are we in Lebanon?" Sara asks the Indian-looking man in front of her.

"Yes," the man whispers, but with doubt in his eyes.

Or is it disbelief? Sara is not sure. The other passengers are all searching the misty darkness outside for signs of deliverance, their backs and necks stiff with suspense, their hands clasping their meagre possessions. Whatever comes next, Sara realizes she won't be facing it alone and this awareness of a shared destiny gives her the strength she needs to keep calm.

She turns to the Ugandan woman and offers her the most reassuring smile she can muster.

acknowledgements

I'm greatly indebted to Zoe Whittall for championing my work. A big thank you to Janice Zawerbny for believing in this collection from the start. I'm incredibly grateful to Sarah MacLachlan, Janie Yoon, and everyone at House of Anansi Press for taking a chance on me and for welcoming me into the fold.

A big thanks to my editor Amanda Lewis for her expert guidance and encouraging words, and for her kindness.

I'm grateful to my parents, my siblings, and my big, beautiful extended family for their love and unfailing support. I'm especially grateful to my parents for their hard work and sacrifice, and for sharing so much of their knowledge and wisdom with me. To my father,

Mohamed Ibrahim, for the love of books you imparted to me, and for answering so many of my research questions. And to my sisters Zamzam and Ferdusa Ibrahim, and Freweyni Getahun, for cheering for me every step of the way.

My eternal gratitude to Dana Jansens, my first, second, and last reader, for believing in me when this book was only an idea, for your infectious enthusiasm and brilliant criticism, for your love and unwavering support.

For their editorial help on early drafts and their friendship, I owe many thanks to Mimy Seble Kassahoun, Rebecca Fisseha, Sara Afa, Lello Omar, Alex Bednar, Robert Delaney, Siobhan Jamison, Charles Shamess, and especially Donna Hughes for her thorough and invaluable feedback.

Thank you to Huda Hassan and Habon Warsame for their great feedback on the story "A Kept Woman," and especially for their help with the Somali words and their spellings.

Michelle Berry, I can't thank you enough for all your help and for your kind words.

It would be impossible to name the many books and articles that have inspired and informed these stories, but I would like to mention one. The background story of the girl killed by her adoptive parents in "Spilled Water" is based on the heartbreaking real story of an Ethiopian adoptee, Hana Williams. The article is titled "Hana's Story," written by Kathryn Joyce and published online on *Slate*.

DJAMILA IBRAHIM was born in Addis Ababa, Ethiopia, and moved to Canada in 1990. Her stories have been shortlisted for the University of Toronto's Penguin Random House Canada Student Award for Fiction and *Briarpatch Magazine*'s creative writing contest. She was formerly a senior advisor for Citizenship and Immigration Canada. She lives in Toronto.

CPSIA information can be obtained
at www.ICGtesting.com
Printed in the USA
LVHW081058140219
607403LV00003BA/3/P